Christian

THE STANTON PACK BOOK 2

KATHI S. BARTON

World Castle Publishing, LLC
Pensacola, Florida
Copyright © Kathi S. Barton 2017
Paperback ISBN: 9781629897653
eBook ISBN: 9781629897660
First Edition World Castle Publishing, LLC, August 7, 2017
http://www.worldcastlepublishing.com
Licensing Notes
Cover: Karen Fuller
Editor: Maxine Bringenberg

Chapter 1

Allie lifted her chin up to the bar seven more times. Dane Stanton had had it put in for her several days ago. Allie was almost finished with her set when she heard the door open behind her. It was going to be another Stanton, she knew it. They'd been in here every day since she'd been brought here. The hospital staff didn't tell her a thing if one of them was in the room with her. It was as if she didn't exist when they were here, and they told everything to whoever was there. Dropping to the floor, she limped over to the chair but didn't sit. She was determined to ignore the person until she was ready. When laughter rang around the room, she looked over at Dane and smiled. Now here was a person she could like.

"How's the leg today?" She told her it was fine, lying through her teeth about it. "Yeah, dumb fuck is doing all right too. His dad finally let him shift this morning, and he's not in the best of humor."

"He's a brute." Dane told her that she was right. "Who the hell talks to someone like that? 'You'll do as you're ordered.'

Like I'm ten or something."

"I think he's regretting it." Allie snorted. "Yes, that's what I thought you'd say. I have something to tell you. Just so you know, I'm only the messenger in this, not the bad guy."

"If it's about the Stantons, I couldn't care less. And for the love of everything holy, please tell Mr. and Mrs. Stanton to stop telling me that they're sorry." Dane told her that they felt bad, and said they'd not raised him to be that way. "Well, I don't know where he got his archaic beliefs, but they're not going to work on me."

"I think he's gotten that." Allie didn't want to sit down. She knew that if she did, she wasn't getting back up easily. "So, if we're through talking about the family and tossing about bullshit, how the fuck is your leg?"

Instead of answering her, she lifted the pants to the scrubs she'd been wearing around the hospital for the last couple of days. She had no idea who had made it so she had a clean pair every morning, but she was glad for them. They covered the worst of the wound on her leg.

"I'm getting better about getting around now. It still hurts like a mother fucker, but the doc told me that had I not been in such good shape in the first place, it could have been a lot worse." Dane touched her fingers along the worst of the stitches. "I'm not going to be able to run for a while."

"That's what I heard too." Allie paced the room. "I have something to tell you. And you're not going to like it. When you leave here, in the morning I heard, you're going to the Stanton house. Your brother said that he couldn't take care of you, what with going out of town again. Perry is going to go on a trip for me, and I said I'd keep an eye on you. But I was called out yesterday too."

"I'm going home." She shook her head. "I'm a grown

woman, Dane. I can take care of myself. I have been for some time now, believe it or not. I can call a cab when I need to…. Why are you shaking your head? I'll be fine."

"Maybe, and I've no doubt that you can care for yourself, but the Stantons, as you know, feel that this is their fault. Or at least some of it. They want to make sure that you're well cared for." Allie said again she was going home. "Brayden is here to take you home tonight instead."

"I'm not going." Brayden came in the room just then, and she told him the same thing she'd told Dane. "I'm not going anywhere with you. I have a very nice rental that I'm going to stay in until my lease is up, then I'm going home."

"The lease has been forfeited." Allie looked at Dane then Brayden. "Christian owns that building and several more downtown. He usually has nothing to do with it, but apparently, he pulled a few strings and got you out of it."

"I don't want to be out of it. I want to live there." She watched as Brayden started collecting her things. When he asked if she wanted to take the water bottle-cup like thing with her, she screamed. "Are you even listening to me?"

"Yes. Great pair of lungs you have on you. But that didn't answer my question." Dane cleared her throat and he winked at her. "I'm trying to be a good deal nicer about this than Christian was going to be."

"He's a dick." Brayden wisely said nothing, but he did continue packing her things for her. Then a nurse came in with a cart for the flowers. "What the hell is going on here? I don't want to fucking go with you."

"You've said that. Several times." She growled at Brayden. "Yeah, since I know you're aware of what we are, you're going to have to do a lot better than that. It comes from the belly. Try it. Just growl like you mean it."

"I don't like you." He was laughing when he took her bag of clothing and other personal items out of the room. Allie looked at Dane. "You can't expect me to live in that house where he is. I can't stand the man."

"He doesn't live there. I mean, he does when he is around, but for the most part, he has an apartment in the city. I'm supposed to find out what you want in a house, but I'm not going to ask you. I like my teeth in my head." She stood up. "Are you ready?"

"Why tonight?" She told her that Christian was out of town. "For how long? Forever? That would suit me just fine if he was."

"He's gone to Cleveland to represent a man on trial for murder." She sat down when Allie did. "So you know, he thinks the guy is guilty, but he wasn't, at the time he said he'd do it, in any position to not go to court for him. He must do three more trials for this guy's father before he can cut ties with him. His father, Landon Hartman, was someone that Christian worked for a long time ago, just out of college, and his contract is very specific as to how many cases he must take. I don't think it's much of a hardship doing things for Landon, but this isn't his usual thing with the man. Repping the stepson, I mean."

"Why are you telling me this?" Dane said nothing, but Allie was sure that she was waiting for her to understand something. "I don't know this man, nor his son."

"Stepson. And yes, you do." Allie stared at her, going over the names of clients that she'd had, friends and other relatives. But none of them rang…. She stared at Dane in horror. "Yes, it's him."

"No." Nodding, Dane said that it was him, the one and only. "He was supposed to be in prison. I don't understand how...does Christian know? Is that why he took his case? To get back at me?"

"I think he knows now, but he didn't when he left here this morning. Christian wouldn't do that, anyway. He might be a dick right now, but that's not his normal way of doing anything. I'm not saying it's you, but something about having you in his life has set him off." Allie said no shit. "Anyway, he's going to try and get out of representing him, based on the fact that you and he are mates."

"No one is going to care. Especially not Park. Mother fuck. Park Davis is...who did he kill? I'm sure that whoever it was, he did it because he had no choice. At least that's what he's going to claim." Dane said that was what he was saying. "Of course he is. Just like he told everyone what he did to me was not his fault. Like I would want someone to rape me. How did you find out?"

"About the rape?" Allie nodded. "I have some friends that found out what he'd been doing time for. I did a couple of searches and found one of his roomies in prison. They were very.... Well, not at first, but they became helpful when I pressured them. He used to brag about it. And as you know, you're not the only co-ed he did that to."

"I know, there were nine of us. And that's only the few that came forward. I still have nightmares about it." Dane said that she would as well. "You're taking me to the Stanton home because of this? You're afraid he'll find out that I'm with Christian, even though I'm not, and come here to get me."

"Something like that. Park's mom will try her best to hold Christian to his contract. She has this unhealthy thing going for her son. Whatever. Christian doesn't think Landon will after he finds out, but I don't have as much trust in people as he does. You may not believe this, but Christian's a good lawyer and rarely loses his cases. But Landon's wife, Joy, the mother of the murderer, doesn't want her little boy in prison again. I get the feeling Landon thinks he belongs there, but his hands are tied. Or so he told Christian." Allie stood but had to hold onto things until her leg started to work for her. "With you being injured, there is a good possibility that he might be able to hurt you more than he did before. I know that you're strong, Allie, and smart, but Park is desperate. Especially if Christian bails on him."

"I just don't know why he'd think that Christian would care if he killed me or not." Dane said nothing. Allie turned to her. "I know about shifters, Dane. I might not have a lot to do with them, but I know that they don't normally treat their other halves the way he did me, nor say the things he did to me. Christian isn't going to tame me or make me heel to his law."

"No, he won't, and I told him that. We all have. But I'd like for you to talk to him. At least give him another chance before you take off." Allie looked at her. "I know you well enough to know that you could be out in plain sight without anyone finding you. Please? As my friend, will you at least give him another chance? It could save both your lives."

"All right. But if he tries that shit again, I'm going to injure him in a way that shifting will not repair. I won't be treated that way." Allie limped around the room, knowing that later she was going to be sore enough that she'd need the drugs again. The bullet might be gone, but the pain of it was still there. "One chance."

~~~

Christian was waiting outside the courtroom when his phone rang. He pulled it out, saw that it was Dane, and nearly put it away. But he remembered what he'd been told, quite painfully, about what would happen to him if he didn't make this work with Allie. Dane, like the rest of his family, had come down hard on him, and he knew that he deserved it. Answering the phone, he waited for her to tell him that Allie had told him to fuck off.

"She said you would have one chance, but I'm not sure that you can handle her. She's a lot meaner than I am." Christian said he'd behave. "You'd better. She's a good friend of mine, and I won't have you fucking that up. All right?"

"You know, I didn't shoot her. The gun went off and that's what did it." He could see her there, lying with her skin sliced open on her leg. All exposed from the bullet that had been, he thought, intended for him. It had entered her thigh deep and gone the length of her leg to her knee before coming out, barely missing her foot. The mark there was small, just like a tear to her instep. From there, it had gone into the ground. She was lucky his dad had been there and he'd not panicked. He had. "I'm not saying I wasn't at fault, but had she not had the gun out and pointed right at me, then she'd be all right now."

"You're not helping." He said he was sorry. "Anyway, she knows what you're doing there and why she's at your parents' house. As you can imagine, she's not all that happy about it, but knows that should he come for her, she isn't in any position to save herself."

"I need to talk to her about what went on. I know what the reports say and I've read over the transcript of the trial, but what I don't understand is, how did he only serve four years of a fifty-year sentence? There wasn't any good behavior on his part. He was just as nasty inside as he'd been out, and Landon swears that he didn't pay to have him released. I believe him." Dane said she was looking into a few things herself. "Just be careful. This is the third time that I've been here with him, and it's getting worse with each one. I don't want to have to do this at all, and I'm hoping the judge will see it that way."

"I don't know how any of that works, but I do know that you can claim that you're related to one of his victims and perhaps that will help." He hoped so as well, but the way that his luck was going, it wouldn't matter. He looked around when she laughed. "I have to tell you, Christian, you're not going to be getting off any easier with Allie than you will me. She might make you go through some major hoops to get back on her good side."

"I was a fool. More than that, I was a fucking idiot. I don't know what came over me." He did, but didn't want to bring it up again. "All I could think was that someone other than me was touching her. And I haven't any idea why that bothered me to the point where I wanted to kill my own brother."

Levi had forgiven him, of course, but he'd yet to forgive himself. He'd never hurt his brother, nor would he have spoken to a woman the way that he had her. Allie had warned him, several times, to back off, and he and his cat, mostly the cat, hadn't cared for that either. When she'd been shot, and hurt him in the process, he'd gone a little wild and hurt Levi again. It took his brother, Brayden, commanding him to stand down before he could get ahold of himself and his beast. Now, not that he blamed her, she was pissed off at him, and he wasn't sure that he could fix this.

His name was called and he told Dane he'd get back to her. As soon as he entered the courtroom, he saw Landon and his wife. Joy wasn't a nice person, and Christian didn't like her at all. He was sure that Landon knew it too.

After shaking hands with the elderly man, he took his seat

at the table. Park would be brought out soon, and he wanted to talk to the judge before that happened. Asking to approach the bench, he let out a long breath before he spoke.

"I would like to recuse myself from this hearing." The judge asked him why and Christian told him what was going on in his life. "My future wife is Allie LaRue. She is currently staying at my parents' home and injured. I cannot, with her being my mate, give Mr. Davis a fair trial. Not with what happened between him and my mate."

"When did you meet her?" He answered all the questions put before him. Even telling the judge that he'd tried calling his office all week but no one would put him through. "I got that you had called, but they'd not tell me what you wanted. I can see now why you wished to speak to me personally."

The judge leaned back in his seat and looked like he was thinking hard on something. The other lawyer, a public defender for the state, asked him if he was serious. That the trial was about to begin.

"I'm well aware of that. I only just found her a few days ago." Stanley was saying how ridiculous this was, that things were too far along for him to do this to him. "I suppose you'd like this to go to trial, and if I win, you'd call foul play and call for a mistrial. I'm trying my best to make sure that doesn't happen."

"Your Honor, you can't—" Judge Piketon told him to shut up. "But sir, this is a murder trial, not a case of rape. I don't understand where the problem lies."

"You wouldn't." Piketon looked at him. "You can prove this? That she's your mate if it comes up? I don't want you in trouble with the law any more than I do for you to have to face your mate if you tell her you got him off."

"I can, sir. As you can imagine, things are a little tense

right now. She's been hurt and I'm here. Not a good way to start a relationship, but my dad and mom are caring for her, and you know them, what sort of people they are." He said that he did. "I just don't think this is a good idea."

"Neither do I. Have a seat gentlemen, I have something to say to the room." Going back to his seat, Christian avoided looking at Landon or his wife. As soon as he was seated, Piketon hit his gavel down on his desk and told them what was going on. "So, as you can see, there will have to be a delay in the trial until such time—"

"No. No, this isn't right." Joy Hartman stood up and turned to him. "No, you have to do this. My husband owns you. You'll take care of this right now."

"Mrs. Hartman, he can't represent your son. There isn't any way for Park to get a—" Joy cut him off, slamming her hands on the seat in front of her. Piketon took exception to that as well. "Now you see here, young lady. I will—"

"You'll make him do this. Tell them, Landon. Tell him that he is going to do this or you'll sue him. He's the best there is, and you said that you never hired anyone that wasn't the best. I want him to make sure my baby doesn't go to prison again." She was told to sit down. "I won't. My husband pays you good money and you'll do as he said. I won't have my baby boy going back to prison for something that he didn't do. Not again. You will make sure of that."

"Mrs. Hartman, I'm going to have to ask you to have a seat. Believe it or not, I'm the one in charge here, and you'll do as I'm telling you or I'll have you tossed out of here." She glared at the judge. "Lady, I've been married to the same wonderful woman for nearly sixty years. That look of yours, it doesn't mean a damned thing to me. Sit down and shut up or I'll have you in the cell next to that baby boy of yours. Now, as I was saying, the hearing is postponed until such time as the Hartmans can find themselves another lawyer or they take on a public defender."

He left them there, not saying another word but leaving them to head to his chambers. Christian started packing up his things, relieved that this part of it was over. When someone touched him on the shoulder, he turned in time to have Joy slug him in the face. He fell back on the table, hitting his head, and just zapped out.

When he woke, he was in the hospital. He knew this because he could smell blood, death, and disease. Then there was the added comfort of having a bed as hard as nails under him, as well as a curtain that kept others out. When he started to sit up, he was pushed back down by a nurse who made his cat curl up around him. Lying down, he asked what had happened.

"I don't know more than you were brought in here a couple of hours ago with a head injury. I was told to stay with you until your wife and family made it here. Which I'm thinking will be soon. I was told that would be about a two-and-a-half-hour trip." He nodded, then held his head. "Yeah, you got yourself a banger there. Just lie still and try not to make me hold you down again. You sure are strong."

"I am. Wait, did you say my wife and family?" She nodded and asked him if he remembered them. "Yes, I do. I just wasn't aware that I had.... I was just making sure you said she was coming. My wife, she's been hurt recently."

"Well, aren't you two a pair?" The nurse asked him if he wanted anything for pain. "You have something on the charts if you want it. It seems like a lot of drugs if you ask me, but the doc, he said you would need more than the average man."

"Yes, I have a high immunity to drugs." Christian

wondered what the doctor was if he knew that he wasn't human. "Will the doctor be back? Soon, I mean?"

"When your family gets here, I'm to give him a call. You want anything to drink? You can have that as well." He said he was fine and laid back on the bed. "All right then. If you promise me that you'll be quiet, I'm going to run to the little girl's room. Don't be getting up, Mr. Stanton, I don't want to have to rope you like a side of beef."

"I'll stay right here." His head was pounding, but he didn't want to take anything for it. If his *wife* was coming, he wanted to be clear headed when he spoke to her. Also, he wondered what had happened after he'd been hit. Other than being here.

The curtain flew back on the rod about twenty minutes later. He knew it was his dad…he'd been yelling his name since he came through the doors. Christian might have called back to him, but the thought of trying to do that with his head pounding like it was didn't appeal to him. So, he waited and now he was here.

"You scared us." Christian said he was sorry as the rest of them crowded in the little area with him. "And so you know, I'm not going to be happy with you if you make that little girl cry. She's hurting pretty badly about now."

"Why did you bring her?" He said that they couldn't leave her at home. "But Dad, I'm all right. She must hurt with her leg injured like it is."

He saw her then, being wheeled back to his area by Judge Piketon. They were talking quietly, laughing at one point too. Christian had to calm his beast when he saw him put his hand out and Allie took it into hers. He had no idea what was wrong with his cat when it came to people touching her, but he had to keep his cool. It was that or go to prison himself for murdering every man that he saw within a foot of her.

Chapter 2

Allie wasn't sure why she was here, other than they didn't want to leave her at the house alone and they needed to see their son. That she didn't understand either…he was a jerk and an ass. But she kept her opinions to herself as they were being kind enough to make sure she had a place to stay.

"Well, Mr. Stanton, we're going to release you with some pain meds. I don't think you'll need them, but I would caution you about shifting right away. You've got yourself a nice bump there, and you'll have to take care not to make yourself ill over this."

"I'll do as you say. I'm going straight home. I've already gotten permission to not go to trial for my client, and this pretty much seals the deal for me anyway." Mr. Stanton asked about charges being pressed against the missus. "I'm not going to do that. She was under a great deal of stress, and I don't want to add to it."

"Well, that's nice of you." She hadn't meant to speak to him, but it was true. She looked away when he smiled at her. "You're still in the shithouse with me, so don't think that got you any brownie points."

"I do owe you a great many apologies. I've not been a nice person." She just looked at him. "I can see by your face that you agree."

"Oh, you got that wrong. I don't just agree with you, but I'd call you a great many more names than just not a nice person. You are so out of the spectrum of not nice that it defies words." She looked away when he laughed. "I'm not kidding you."

"No, I can see that. And as much as you'd like to hurt my feelings—which again, I don't blame you—I deserve it and more." He sat up in the bed and closed his eyes. "Damn, but that hurts."

"You have a concussion, you idiot. Sit still like you were told." He laughed, but didn't move anymore. She looked at his mom and asked if she could just find a hotel here. It would be easier since she had a big baby at home. "I don't need anyone to wait on me hand and foot. I get around fairly well."

"No." She looked at him, ready to tear him a new ass when he spoke again. "No, please don't leave me. I want you close, and if you're not, I'll leave home to find you. You heard the doctor, I need to be taken care of."

"I think what he said was for you to take it easy. There was no mention of you being cared for. You're a big boy. I think you can manage whatever you need." He grinned, his head still back on the bed and his eyes closed. "Are you in that much pain?"

"Yes." She believed him and moved closer to the bed. She had no idea why, but it hurt her in ways she couldn't describe that he was in pain. "Can I hold your hand? I know that I've messed up, but I would really like some comfort right now."

"I don't like you." But she put her hand on his to have

him curl his fingers into hers. "Don't get used to this. I am not happy with you."

"I won't. But I do thank you." She didn't say anything more, but listened to the rest of them speaking about the trial and other things that were going on in their lives. "Allie, do you think that when we get back home, that you could please come to my apartment? No pressure or anything, and I promise not to bully you ever again. But I like living on my own, and I don't want to impose on my parents any more than I have to."

"I doubt they'd think of you as a burden." He squeezed her hand but said nothing. "Look, I don't know if you realize this or not, but I'm not very good around people. Men especially. They...since Park, I avoid them completely if I can. Mostly, I do what I do to teach people how to defend themselves against bullies."

"I can understand that. And I read the report on what he did to you and the others." She started to jerk her hand away from his, but he held her tight. "Don't. I'm sorry. I know that you were hurt by him, and to be honest with you, I'm glad to be done with him. His stepdad is a nice man, but Park is a bastard."

"Mr. Hartman came to see me in the hospital. He took care of the bills for the stay, as well as the therapist that I still see occasionally. I even get a card from him, for my birthday and Christmas." He asked her if it was hurtful. "No. I mean, I thought it was at first. It was like he was rubbing salt in the wounds. But his words were sincere, and so was his pain at what had happened to me."

"I don't think when he married Joy that he knew Park came as a package deal. At least that's what I get from him when I go to court or meetings with him. And today, Joy is the one that put me here." She asked him why he'd not pressed charges. "Because I like him. It has nothing to do with her. And Landon would be the one to suffer."

As he laid there, his eyes closed, she thought of Park and what he'd done to her. It had been horrific. Over three days he'd kept her tied to a wall, where he had repeatedly raped her and sodomized her. To this day, even though it had been five years, she still woke in a cold sweat and had to lay in her bed for hours just to get her body to calm down.

"Are you all right?" She looked at him, her mind wrapped up in her memories. "Look at me, Allie. Look into my eyes. Allie, I have you. Breathe, baby. Breathe."

She couldn't, couldn't even think above the wild pounding of her heart. Suddenly the sting to her face brought her out of it and she looked at Dane, then at Christian. He told her he had her and wrapped her up in his arms.

"I'm sorry." Sobbing, thinking how she'd made a fool of herself, she tried to extract herself from his arms. It felt good, but she was too emotional to have him see her this way. But instead of letting her go, he held her tighter. "He was there. I think this has brought back all of this."

"Of course it did. No hard feelings, right?" She took Dane's hand and told her no, no hard feelings. "You scared me a bit there. And I don't normally scare easily. Are you okay?"

"Most of the time, no. But I thank you. I might have embarrassed you all more had you not helped."

Dane started to speak but was cut off by the nurse with a wheelchair. They were making their way out to the large van when she realized that she didn't have any idea where she was going. So, waiting until they were ready, she stayed back.

It was then that she saw the woman coming toward them

all. She, of course, knew who Joy Hartman was. The woman had been in the courtroom every day of the trial against her son. Allie looked around and no one was paying any attention to what would be a fight. Yelling would do no good, she knew that. The Stantons were a very loud group. So, she did the only thing she could think of and put her fingers in her mouth and let go of the shrillest whistle she could muster. Everyone turned to her.

All she needed to do was point. Dane turned first, then the rest followed suit. She was surprised when two of Christian's brothers came to her and stood in front of her, like a human shield. She could still see the woman, but she did feel a great deal better with the added protection.

"Joy? What are you doing here?" Christian hadn't yet been helped into the van, so he spoke to her calmly and softly. "You almost missed me if you meant to tell me goodbye. I'm going home to be—"

"I'm not here to tell you goodbye, because you don't have my permission to leave us like this. People are making up things about my son again, and I want you to get it taken care of. He isn't like they're painting him to be. And it doesn't matter to me about you having some sort of girlfriend. She can't be all that wonderful. Not like my son is to me." He looked where she did, right at Allie. "This is the person that you're going to marry, Christian? Tell me that it's all a joke and I'll believe you. This woman is a liar. She told lies about my son and he was sent to prison. You can't be serious, Christian. Her of all people? Why would you do something so mean to me?"

"I'm not doing a thing to you, Joy. She's going to be my wife." She'd not said yes to any such thing, but thought it wise to let that go for now. "And according to the law and a jury of his peers, she didn't lie and your son was sent to prison for his actions. We did talk about this, Joy. I explained to you what would happen before the trial went to court. I wasn't here to defend him, but I did explain to you what might happen should he be found guilty."

Allie looked at Christian. He'd not been in the courtroom, not ever while the trial was going on the first time. She would have remembered him. She knew that he had a good solid relationship with Mr. Hartman, and wondered why he had not gone to court then. Not that it was any of her business. She just wanted to get out of there. Now.

"I need you to come back and do this for me. For Park. He's a good boy, and I don't know why everyone is always accusing him of things he's not capable of. And the few things that he has done, those were things that every child does. Just come back to the courthouse with me, tell the judge that you made a mistake, and then we'll work on getting rid of this woman for you. You do not want to hook your sails to her, Christian."

Mrs. Stanton came to stand with her, behind her sons. And when she took her hand in hers, Allie wanted jerk away and tell them that she'd not wanted this in the first place. Joy started talking before she made a fool of herself.

"Christian, come on. The judge might change his mind as well."

"No." Allie wondered if Joy was used to having people tell her that, but Christian didn't seem to be satisfied with just that and continued. "I'm not going to go back to the courtroom for any reason. I can't believe after you slugged me that you'd even think that I would. Now be on your way before I call the police and change my mind about pressing charges for your hitting me."

She left, but not before spitting in Allie's direction. It wasn't that bad, really, but someone might have thought she carried some disease the way that the men in front of her reacted. Their cats, just there on the surface, were ready to take them over, but they seemed to have a great deal of control over them. She might not have done so well, herself. Allie backed from them and into the wall. The sooner she was on her own, the better.

~~~

Christian watched Allie. She hadn't said a word since they got into the van. She was sitting next to him on the big seat, her leg across his lap, but she might as well have been in the other car with the rest of his family for the distance that he felt between them. Trying once again to engage her into come conversation, perhaps to find out what was wrong, he told her about their home and where it was.

"I've put a bid in on a house that isn't far from my parents' house. I did it a few days before I met you. It's across the street from Brayden's. All the houses in the area where we'll live are big homes. Most of them are from the turn of the century, but we've all done upgrades on them. More bathrooms and closets. I think it's Colton's home that—"

"I have an apartment, the way I like it, and since you stepped in where it was none of your concern, I don't have anywhere to call my own while I'm here. Under contract, nothing to do with you." He nodded and asked her if there was room for him in it. "You just told me you have a house. That it's huge. Why would you want to stay in my one bedroom apartment?"

"Because you're there." She looked away from him and he was tempted to jerk her back around to speak to him. He looked in the rearview mirror and caught the reflection of his

25

mom. *She's mad at me.*

I would say that's a good assessment. What do you think she's upset about? He said he was breathing. *That could be a bit of it, but I'm thinking it has more to do with the fact that she was called a liar, and instead of saying anything when Joy told you she'd get rid of her for you, you walked away.*

I didn't want to engage with a madwoman. His mom asked him who he was protecting. *I don't know. Her. Me. Mom, she's stubborn.*

Yes, I agree with you on that one. She's very hurt, too. I'm not saying you're fully responsible, never that, but you brought things up that I'm betting she has to work very hard at keeping down. Christian looked at Allie as his mom continued. *Did you by chance read the entire report on her? Not just the court paperwork, but all of it?*

No. I mean, there really wasn't much time. I had planned on it when I returned from this hearing. I had no idea when I left what was going on with her. His mom told him to make it a priority. Or better yet, to ask her about her life. *She's hurting already, won't that make it worse?*

No, I don't think so. How do you feel when you get a chance to unload a problem you're having? He told her that he usually felt better. *Yes, I'm sure that she will as well. Take her to your home, don't do anything stupid, and talk to her. I swear to you, Christian, it will go a good deal better for you if you do.*

The rest of the trip home, he held her hand, spoke to her when he thought of something, but really, was thinking about what he was going to say to her about them. And he knew that he'd have to talk to her. He'd been an ass and a dick, and that was only the beginning of what was happening. Just as he was going to ask if she was hungry, that they were stopping for lunch, she turned to him.

"Do you suppose that Joy will come after you?" Christian asked her why she'd do that. "She's not a very nice person, as you've pointed out. And from my experience with her, she doesn't like to be told no, nor does she like when things don't go her way. Even if it is all on her."

"I'm sure that she's fairly levelheaded, and once she thinks about this, she'll feel foolish." He didn't believe that, not after today, and revised his statement. "You know, you might be right. I've never been punched by someone before the trial took place. She might just be unhinged enough to come for us both. And I'm not just saying that to keep you close, but she is off her rocker a little."

"That's what I was thinking. I've taken a great many classes in college about people's behavior, and while I'm not an expert on it, I don't think she's got all her screws tightened up." Levi, who was riding with them, turned and asked what she meant. "Well, who does that? I mean, who punches an attorney in a courtroom full of armed men? Or for that matter, cameras out the wazoo, a judge, as well as a handful of other witnesses? It sounds to me like she doesn't care about anything but herself and her needs. Or Park's. She is insane with her need to protect him, and he's a grown assed man too."

"And an idiot as well. Plus, I'd never say this to his family, but I do believe he killed that man purely because he could. However, Landon, he's stable and secure. Do you suppose he'd be able to keep her in check?" Allie told Levi that usually no, but this could be different. "But you don't think so, do you?"

"No, I don't." Levi looked at Christian as Allie continued. "I was working with a woman once. She'd been robbed at gunpoint on her way home from work. The robber took the

27

deposit and all her cash she had on her. Her self-esteem was tested the most, because the company that she worked for placed the blame at her feet and they fired her. So, I worked with her, showing her not how to hurt someone, but to defend herself when she was in a situation that she couldn't get out of. Her husband was calm, cool, and collected. He came to each class, even going as far as paying for them up front. Then two weeks after she was finished with the classes, she murdered her wonderfully supportive husband because he tried to get her to back off when the postal worker didn't deliver the package that she'd been waiting on. It was a gift to him for his support. It arrived later that night from a different carrier."

"You're saying that you think, based on this, that Joy is on a hair trigger and might snap?" She told him that she already had done that today. "Yes, but her son is going down for murder. Do you think that might have been a contributing factor in this?"

"Oh yes. She thinks he's perfect, and anything he's ever gotten caught at, which I'm sure that there are many things that we don't even know about, she's been able to blame it on everything and everyone else. Never him. Plus, there is the fact that he'd already gone down for the rape of seventeen college women. Three of which have committed suicide, and two more are in a mental hospital." He wondered if she'd spent any time in one, and decided that he was going to read that report if he had to do it all night long. "And there his mom was, shouting to anyone that would listen that her little boy would never do anything like that. Never harm anyone, that he was more than likely fending them off him because he's such a good boy with money. But once someone pointed out all the evidence after his trial, she did snap and nearly killed the man by hitting him with a tire iron. And like you just did, he didn't press charges because she was apparently distraught as well as losing her little boy."

"Christ." Allie nodded and leaned her head back on the seat as he thought about what she'd just told him. "I had no idea that that had happened. When your trial against him was going on, I was away on another one. Landon had me looking into some contracts that he was thinking of signing. But had I been there, I'm not sure that the verdict would have come out any differently."

She sat there for a few more minutes, none of them talking much. His mom and dad were talking about the picnic that was coming up; Levi laid back on his seat and closed his eyes. Christian asked Allie if she was in much pain. Instead of answering him, she changed the subject. He went with it, to help her out.

"Have you ever just wanted to go out into the woods and sit down? I mean, not for any other reason than to simply enjoy the quiet?" He told her that there were times when he did that, as his cat. "Do you scare away the animals? I don't know that much about your kind. I know that you're a cougar and you shift, but nothing more."

"Dane is an elite. Do you know what that is?" She told him that she didn't. "She can shift into anything that has a heartbeat. She might be able to shift into other objects as well, but so far, she said she's not keen on finding out. Dane has had her DNA played with, and she is very enhanced."

"Nelson's, right?" He nodded and asked her how she knew. "Dane and I have been friends for some time, and we talk. Not a lot, because as you know, neither of us are the gabby type. While I know that she's a shifter, I don't know what kind or anything much about it, except that she can shift and keep her clothing with her."

"So can Brayden. He found that out quite by accident a couple of days ago when he was out in the yard and his clothing came back when he became a man again." She smiled and he did as well. "She has some freaky abilities too. Brayden isn't ready to try any of those out just yet, so we don't know if he has them as well."

"Will you change me? If I go home with you, will you make me a cat too?" He wasn't sure how to answer that, so waited until she clarified. "I don't know if I want anything like that. I know that the sex part is intense and that you're possessive, but I'm not sure if I want to be able to shift. I have enough going on in my life right now, and that sounds too complicated."

"It's not, but I understand. And yes, I'd like to convert you, but we can live a long and happy life—if you give me another chance—without you changing." She nodded. "I know nothing about you. I mean, you don't me either, but I'd like to learn."

"I have a brother, Perry, as you know. Our parents, Heath and Allison LaRue, are both living, but we rarely see them anymore. Not for lack of trying, but they were young parents and decided that when Perry and I were out on our own, they wanted to travel and see the world. I don't know how much they've seen of it. They don't have a lot of money; their camper is about as old as I am, and my dad is handicapped. He had a terrible accident at work once and lost both his legs from the knees down. I love them, but I don't see them much."

"My parents have been together for a long time. Since childhood, as a matter of fact. They knew what they were to each other when they were about ten, and grew up and fell in love. I love them very much, as well as my brothers." She asked him if they'd always had money. "Yes, though they

30

never gave us everything we wanted. If we wanted a car, we worked for it, plus, paid the insurance and upkeep. College was paid for, but we had to work for anything we wanted while there. Not books or food, but fun. I don't think any of us did anything but our best while away, and all returned home as much as we could. Brayden was gone a lot before meeting Dane, but he's here now and we're loving it."

"I see Perry every day. He doesn't live with me, but he is in the same apartment complex as me. And we've never lived in a house. Perry did for a little while...he was married once, but his wife passed away when they were first married — car accident — and he sold the house and moved into an apartment after that." He said he was sorry. "She was wonderful for us. Very organized, and cooked like a dream. They didn't have any children, and I think that Perry is saddest about that. He wanted to wait for a while."

"Do you want children?" She didn't answer him, so he did what she had, changed the subject. "When I was in college, I had this professor that thought that you should be prepared for a test at a moment's notice. Pens, not pencils for them. Blue, not black, though I don't understand that one, and we had to have notes. Each test that he gave was open notes...not book, but notes."

"You more than likely aced them all." He just smiled at her. "You did, didn't you? You are that smart?"

"I am, but I didn't always ace them. Once I missed one. But hush now, and let me tell you my story." She giggled and he lost his train of thought. "You are beautiful. Has anyone told you that before?"

"The story." He nodded and smiled at her. "You aren't that charming, Mr. Stanton. Marginally so, but not all that much."

31

"Thank you." He grinned. "The story, yes. Well, I was sitting in the classroom and he comes in with this stack of papers. We know the drill, and we pulled out notebooks and pens and just started on them. I like to read each question and answer. Some people...Brayden, he likes to read over the test and then answer them. I was nearly to the last page when I noticed I was the only one in the room. I answered the last questions and took the paper up to him. He just shook his head and gathered up his things and left. I did ace that one."

Levi started laughing. "Yeah, you did, but it wasn't your test." She asked him what he meant. "It was a chemistry test, and the class he was in was for corporate law. He passed a test on a class that he wasn't taking."

"Yes, well, he did tell us to be prepared for anything." She was laughing hard when they pulled into the restaurant parking lot. He held her leg when the rest of them got out, and waited for the doors to close. "Are you all right, Allie? You need anything?"

"I don't know." He nodded and told her that he understood. "Do you? I don't. I have no idea what I'm doing or what is happening. I'm exhausted, hurting, hungry, and I'm confused. I don't even know who to ask for help."

"When we get home, I'll pamper you. Give you something for the pain. Right now, I can make sure you're fed. And as for being confused? So am I. But I think, more than anything, we can work this out. If you'll give me a chance." She said she wasn't sure. "Well, that's better than a flat-out no."

Chapter 3

Park sat in the chair and waited for his mom. She was late. Again. He looked around at the other losers and wondered why he was being subjected to such lowlifes. Park thought that there should be a holding place for people like him. Moneyed.

When he saw his mom, he huffed at her. Picking up the phone on his side of the cell, he waited for her to do the same.

"Well? Can you tell me what the fuck happened the other day?" She pulled out her notes, something that he never understood about her. Why write shit down? If it was important, you'd remember. Otherwise, who gave a good fuck? "Why did I get all the way to the courthouse then have to be brought back without getting out of here?"

"The attorney, he found himself a slut that you were supposed to have raped." He asked her what that had to do with his situation. "Well, conflict of interest, I guess. She is the love of his life, apparently. Fucker. I tried to talk to him but he was determined to go on his way, bastard, and Landon wouldn't do anything about it either. We pay that man good money, and he does this to my baby boy."

"Mom, you do realize that I do not belong here, correct? I want you to tell Landon that I want him to pay that man whatever he wants to get me out of here. I'm not happy, and he will know what that means." He looked at the guard when he cleared his throat. He knew that whatever he said was being recorded, so he had to think about how to word things. "I didn't do whatever they said I did. This is just their way of keeping me down. I'm a good man."

He wasn't, and everyone that encountered him knew that. He was a bastard, a murderer, and he *had* raped all those women. It was what he did. Whatever he wanted, to whomever he wanted, and there wasn't anyone to tell him no. He looked at his mom again.

"Park, I'm doing the best I can. Landon is being very stubborn about this. He claims that he told you that he wasn't going to be at your beck and call anymore, and that he was cutting you off. And even me giving him the treatment hasn't worked either." She pushed out her lower lip, something that usually got her whatever she wanted. But not from him. "I'm going to try and go to Christian again, but he put out a restraining order against me. Just because I might have hit him in my anger."

"You hit him?" He laughed. "Well, good old Mom sure has some spunk, don't you? Did you knock him on his ass? God, I wish I had been there. To see you getting your panties all twisted up." His voice turned harsh. "But I couldn't. Because you know why? My fucking lawyer bailed on me and you allowed it."

"Park, honey, I didn't want him to leave. He just did, and took that slut with him." His mom looked to her right and then nodded. Park supposed she was getting reprimanded by the guard. "Park, we only have about three minutes left. I'll come back tomorrow and see you. Do you need anything?"

He didn't bother answering, instead he got up and shuffled back to the door. The chains on his wrists and ankles prevented him from just storming out of the room. Park wasn't sure where his mom had failed him, but she was going to pay as soon as he got out of here. To think that she'd left him to rot in here for the last week without any kind of assurances that he was going to be released soon pissed him off.

His cell was just as he'd left it. No one had come in and made his bed, cleaned his commode, or even the mess that he'd made last night when he'd been given that crap they called a meal.

Park wanted to have his food catered, meals made especially for him. Steak and baked potato, grilled tomatoes, and a glass of the best wine. As he sat on the lumpy excuse for a mattress, he bemoaned the fact that no one was helping him. Not a single person, other than his mom, had come to see him. A whole week and none of his friends had made an appearance.

He wondered if they knew where he was. Most wouldn't be surprised, but the ones he called real friends, they'd be as outraged as he was. Damn it, he was missing out on the best parties and shit going down.

"Someone is going to pay for this." He tried to remember the attorney's name. Stand? No, that wasn't it. Stand something. Park laid back on the bed, resting his head against the wall. Stanton. That was it. The name also triggered another memory. College.

Park laughed. "So, you were the goody two shoes that turned me in for making a little extra on the side? Jesus, you'd think you might have learned something about me back then."

He'd paid nearly five grand for delivery of alcohol every day. Sharing with his buddies might have been a mistake. It had been necessary for him to take bigger chances with having his favorite stock delivered to his room just to keep his buddies happy. Drinking all night had led to him missing classes and doing poorly on tests. Then, after a time, he'd been tossed out on his ass without anything to show for his stay there. It was likely about the time that he realized that having money couldn't do you shit if you were at school.

Stanton had turned him in to the dean. Apparently, Park having late night parties had been bothering him when he was trying to study or sleep. Who the fuck studied when they could have been drinking and having a grand time? Stanton did, he supposed. And now, he was back again.

When lunch time came, he didn't even bother talking to the cop that brought it. The fucker didn't like him questioning his every move, nor did he like when Park suggested to him that he get better treatment. The last time he had argued with one of them, he'd been put in a room all alone and had not gotten any food for hours. He had nearly gone insane sitting in the dark without anyone to talk to. Park needed to be social.

Stanton was his attorney, and he needed to get in touch with him to tell him what would happen if he didn't get him out of here. Just the week before he'd killed Oliver, Landon had told him that he was done with him, but that didn't mean that he should be left to rot in this place just because Landon had gotten a burr up his ass.

"You're a grown man, Park, and should be making your own way in the world. I'm finished bailing you out, and there won't be any more charges made to my accounts. Your mother's either. You are both on a budget." Park just laughed. "You think this is some sort of joke?"

"I do, as a matter of fact. You think that my mom is going to stand for that? Doubtful. She runs the roost and you know it." Park had thought it was very funny that his stepfather was thinking that in any way this was going to work. "While you're making rules that I have no intentions of following, I need some cash. A couple of grand, if you have it. If not, give me a card; I'll make do with that."

Landon only sat there. Park was pissed, but he didn't let him know that. Instead, he stood up, slicing his hand over Landon's desk, knocking everything off. Leaving the office, he heard Landon laughing and wondered what drugs he was on. He'd just broken some of his shit. But it wasn't until that afternoon, spent in one of his favorite shops, that he realized Landon had done just what he said. And his mom's card didn't work either when he tried to pay for the suit he wanted to buy. Not even telling the man to go ahead and send the bill to Landon had worked. He had called him already, he'd told Park, and Landon said he wasn't going to pay for it.

And that had been the beginning of him being put in here. A little misunderstanding between friends. Oliver had wanted him to pay him for the damage he'd done to his car, and he didn't have it. So, he decided to take it out of his hide, whatever the fuck that had meant.

Oliver wasn't a friend. He was just some guy that he hung out with when there wasn't anyone else around. His parents bought him off all the time...thus him having a brand-new car. But Park had driven too close to the curb and the pole there, and had done some major damage to it. Oliver wanted him to pay the deductible, even though Park knew his parents would.

Once he started swinging his fists at him, Park had pulled out the gun he always had on him. One shot, that's all it had taken to kill him. Park hadn't even meant to kill him, only to make him understand he was the better man, but Oliver had lunged and he had fired at the same time. Obviously not his fault, however, the police hadn't seen it his way and had brought him here.

"Overreacting about nothing that was their concern." He thought about his mom and how she'd failed him as well. "No one understands the complexity of me. How delicate I am and how I need to have…no, deserve, special treatment."

Park had been about ten when his own father had died. Well, that wasn't quite right either. He was dead, yes, but he didn't just die. Park had poisoned him. With his mom's help, too. Slowly, over the course of a month. Dad had been his first attempt at murder, and he found that he was good at it. Not to mention how much fun it had been. Christ, he had really enjoyed it. And since then, he'd perfected himself to the point where no one would know it was him. Until that bitch.

Park had killed his first woman one night when she wouldn't shut up after he decided he wasn't going to pay her when she left him hanging. Coming once hadn't been enough, and she didn't want to give it out anymore until he paid for his first fuck. Well, he'd cleared that up quickly enough by knocking her in the head several times with a cinder block. Then after that, he became less selective and had a great deal more fun.

Then that one bitch had gone and turned him in to the police. When Park had called his mom and Landon, that hadn't gotten him anything but a half-assed attorney that didn't do shit for him. And no matter how many times he'd told the piece of shit that he wasn't going to prison, he'd ended up there anyway. All because the last woman had gotten it in her head to tell on him. The next time he took a woman to his lair, he was going to kill her at the end of her stay and not let her speak against him. Not ever again.

He didn't know names. It wasn't like he was forming a friendship with them when he took them. They were a fuck… that was it. Or a few fucks, or whatever else he had wanted. When he tired of them, or found another one that took his fancy, he'd cut them loose out in the woods and then start over. The women, he thought, were better off for having known what a real man wanted. Most of the time, anyway.

"Now I'm here again, and by no fault of my own. Just some cocksucker wanted money from me. It's not fair."

Park got up and paced the room, ignoring the food that had been brought to him. There were more important things to take care of than eating at the moment. Park began pacing the floor, trying to remember anything about the bitch from the courtroom at his first trial.

He did remember her voice. It had been pretty. The way that she'd begged him to leave her alone. For him to let her go. But he enjoyed the voice better after that. Her begging had gotten her nowhere, of course, but he had enjoyed it tremendously. Park frowned. She'd not screamed. Not one time, no matter what he'd done to her. What she looked like started to form in his mind. Her body first, when he'd cut her loose. Then her face when he'd been done with her. As those details returned, he remembered the way her face had been cut and bleeding. The bandages she wore in the courtroom had made him recall her eyes when she'd stared at him. Detestation and abhorrence toward him. It had startled him, he remembered, the way that she looked, as if given the chance she'd kill him. A woman? Killing him? Not fucking likely.

Remembering every detail about her, he began to see

her in the courtroom. Other people were there too, but this woman, she'd had notes, drawings of him, as well as details that he'd not thought of.

She had described his clothing. The way that his breath sometimes smelled of mint. There were details about the tattoo he had on his shoulder, and the one that he had on his back. She had even written down what he'd fed her and the amount that she'd been given. This was all memories, his attorney had said, but then he had to show his tattoos, and that had nearly sealed the deal for him. But the real kicker had come when she told the courtroom that he had a scar on his dick, one he'd gotten when he'd been a baby. That had been enough to convict, his attorney told him later.

Her voice had been rough, too, in the courtroom. He'd cut her neck at one point, holding a knife to her throat when he'd taken her. She walked with a limp then; her leg had been cut badly as well, from the ropes that he'd used to tether her. Yes, he remembered that. He'd used a broken bottle on her skin too, marring what he had thought of as perfection. Because to him, he could be the only one that was perfect. He'd been trying his best to mark her so that every time she saw the wounds, then later the scars, she'd remember him and what they'd had before.

Park picked up his tray and poked at the sandwich there. A ham on white. White, for Christ's sake. There was a bag of chips...baked, not even fried. He had been given a bottle of water. Not even a selection of the kind of water that he drank. They didn't give him a menu to choose from either. He took what they gave him or starved, he'd been told the second day.

Park was tempted to just throw it at the wall again, but he didn't want to be hosed down when they saw it. They had used a fire hose on him, knocking him into the walls, which had torn into his skin harshly and had torn his clothing nearly off him. That hadn't been nice at all, and he wanted to never experience that shit again.

Making a mark on the wall, he was counting the days. For every mark on the wall, someone was going to pay. As soon as he figured out how to do it, he was going to kill the bitch. No one fucked with him and got away with it.

~~~

Christian was in his office when Betty came in to tell him that someone was there to see him. He asked her if he'd missed something. She smiled. Betty had worked for him for years, and this smile was one that he didn't witness often enough. She was genuinely happy.

"No, he doesn't have an appointment, but I think it might be good for you to see him. Landon is here." He looked at the door and back at her, and Betty laughed. "He's alone. And he told me to tell you that Joy doesn't know he's here."

"I don't like her." Betty said she didn't care much for her either. "Yes, well, she's a shark, and her son is a monster. Not anyone that I would have thought he'd marry."

"Don't I know that. Would you like for me to send him in?" He told her to go ahead. "Oh, before I forget, Allie called. She didn't want you to be disturbed, but she said that the furniture that you ordered is there and she's having it set up in the rooms. Your brothers are there with your mom and sister-in-law. The leap is helping too, I guess."

"Tell her that I'll call her later, after this meeting." She left him and Landon filled the doorway. He wasn't a big guy, but he projected an image that made you think he was ten times the size of most men. "Hello, Landon. What can I do for you? If this has to do with the trial yesterday, I'm sorry about that. I found my mate and she is connected to Park."

"I know. After the courtroom was dismissed, I had someone search into the information and found out who she was. Wonderful young woman, by the way. And the connection to Park...I'm so sorry about that." He asked him to have a seat. When Landon sat, he continued. "I'm here on another matter. It does concern Park, but not that. I want him taken out of my will. Joy as well. Also, I'd be obliged if you were to file divorce papers."

"That bad, huh?" Christian started pulling out paper to make notes on. "The will won't be a problem. I can do that in a few minutes. Divorce? Well, there is a little more paperwork involved in that, but no trouble if you have the time. We're a no-fault state, but that doesn't mean that she won't fault you."

"Yes, yes. I figured that, and I do have the time if you do. But I want this done now. Today. And filed just as quickly... the sooner the better. And as she signed that prenup, I don't have to mess with finding how much more she wants to drain me after this. I knew she was trouble, has been for the last few months, but hitting you and then making demands of me.... Did you know that she wanted me to mortgage my family home to pay for someone to let her son out? I'm still trying to figure out who did it for her in the first place." Christian had an idea but he didn't voice it. But Landon seemed to understand. "I'm thinking that she's taken out a loan against my life insurance policy to pay someone to make this happen. And full payment is going to be me being dead."

"You want that changed as well?" He said that was an excellent idea. "Who do you want to be the executor?"

"You." Christian looked up at him, ready to object when Landon asked him to let him explain. "I don't know anyone else that I can trust to make the donations that I have lined up. You will, of course, be paid from the estate and insurance, but

I want to make some donations to some of the charities that you have working in town."

"I can do that, but we'll have those in writing too. Then no one thinks I made you do anything." He handed him notarized paperwork and Christian looked it over. "All right, this takes care of that. And the rest?"

"Yes. That too. I want you to take care of a few things for me on a personal level as well. Now wait before you jump the gun. I have a great deal of money…you do as well. So, I'd like for you to set up a trust fund for the city to go with the other things that are going on. Like the shelter. And a college fund for the high school. That list is with the other envelope."

It took them several hours to get through all the paperwork. The will was witnessed by Betty so that in the event that he couldn't get it filed today, it would be in effect. There were other signatures needed as well, and Brayden and his father witnessed for them when he asked them to come in. By three, he had it all set to be filed in the morning, first thing, if no one could make it in today.

"Anything else?" Landon leaned back in his chair and smiled. "You old devil you, what have you got up your sleeve now? Something fun, I'm betting."

"Yes. Though I don't think your mate will be all that thrilled about it." Christian waited. "I want to make her the benefactor of my estate, the homes that I have, cars, and jewels. She…I know what Park did to her. I read over the court scripts and I was there to witness it all. To hear that poor girl talking about the things he'd done to her…well, I would never wish that on my own worst enemy. And I've seen the other women too. Allie no more deserved that than they did, but she is the one that brought him to justice."

"Why? I mean, I'm not going to tell her, not if you don't

want me to, but why are you singling her out?" He told him. "I see. You want Park and Joy to know who got the estate and why. You are going to be causing trouble long after you're gone, aren't you?"

"Yes. It's the best I can do from the grave." Christian made notes as Landon continued. "He killed that man, no doubt about it, and for some reason, I have no idea why, he's going to get off. Someone—my wife, I'm betting—will help that happen. She'll get desperate now that she knows that the cards are cut off, as well as the bank. No money, nothing starting three days ago. Joy seems to think she can un-sex me into giving in. And not to be crass, but I'm not the least bit upset about that either."

"I'm sorry, Landon, I truly am." Landon told him not to worry about it. There were worst things in life. "Yes, but you're a good man who doesn't deserve this. I'm assuming that you're taking precautions to keep you safe."

"I am. I've decided to hire that girl of yours and her brother. Allie is going to be my bodyguard for the next several weeks if I can talk her into it. And that brings up another thing I wanted to talk to you about. You should convert her. Soon." He said that they'd not had a lot of time to even become mates yet. "Yes. I guess with her being hurt and all this other shit going on your romance has gone to the side. But you need to work on that too. In my opinion, you couldn't do any better than Allie LaRue. Make damned sure you fix this with her."

"How would you suggest I get around to that, Landon? I have old men coming into my office and making large changes to their will. Divorcing a woman he more than likely should never have married." They both laughed hard over that. "I have a plan for this weekend to take her out to dinner. Then we'll talk. I have her staying at my new house now, and I think that's an accomplishment. And her brother, he approves."

"Yes, you need to get the family involved in this. Never hurts to have backup when you need it. Your mom, she's a good woman, and there isn't any better doctor around than your daddy. Did I tell you that he was there when my Julie got sick? Held both our hands through the whole ordeal." Christian remembered Julie Hartman. She'd been a wonderful person, and it nearly broke Landon when she passed away. "Enough of this morose talk. I want you to go out, have a wonderful time, and bring that girl back happy as a clam in a salty bath."

After he left, Christian worked on what he needed done for the man. The filing of the divorce papers was finished first, along with the will changes so that Betty could get them to the courthouse. Calling him from there, she told him that she'd gotten them filed. He called Landon on his cell to let him know that it was a done deal.

"Good news all around. Hire me a man to go out and deliver it. I'm making a call now to have things changed up at home. Should be an eventful day all around for us." He told him to be careful. "Plan on it. I'm going to go on an extended vacation for a few weeks if I can manage to stay out of trouble. Should be nice in France about now."

Christian was laughing as he hung up the phone. The man was going to be all right, and out of reach for anything that might befall him. Lucky for Landon, he could just go where he wanted when he wanted and not worry about something as mundane as packing a bag.

The rest of the afternoon was spent finishing up paperwork and making calls. At four-thirty he was almost out the door when his phone rang. It was the police.

"Mr. Stanton? It's Blake from the station house. We have

a Mr. Williams here. He's been injured." Christian asked if he needed representation. "Yes, sir. And I'm thinking you might be the man for it. He was serving Mrs. Hartman and he got his head hit with one of them poles they use to get clothing down from the high racks at the mall. We've arrested her and she's on her way to county now, but Mr. Williams is headed to the emergency room and he's wanting to press charges. You game?"

"Tell him I'm on my way. That he's not to say anything more. Thanks for calling me." He said it was his pleasure all the way around. "Did she do anything else?"

"Nothing we can't just slap onto her sentences. He found her at a pretty store in the mall. She was having an issue with her credit cards and we'd been called in beforehand. We got there just in time to pull her off him before she did some real damage. Williams must have heard about it on the scanner, and that was how he ended up there serving her. When he got there, it was like she'd been holding it in and let him have it. A few of the clothing racks won't be the same, but like I said, she's gonna pay for them somehow. Oh, since we're doing this new camera thing on our uniforms, him serving her has been officially recorded and logged. He did his part just before the ambulance arrived whilst we held her. Best time I've had in a bit and a while."

"Thank you. And I'm glad that someone got a kick out of it. Tell him I have to make one stop then I'll be there, and that I'm sorry about this." Blake said it was fine, he'd enjoyed himself too. "I bet he did. I'm thinking she didn't come in easy for you."

Blake laughed. "No, she did not. But I tell you, she needs to learn that four big men can subdue the best of them. She didn't like it, but we got her to cooperate right fast before it was done. Like I said, she's gonna be paying for a few things out of her own pocket soon."

Chapter 4

Allie wasn't sure what to do with all this furniture. There were three couches that had to go into the seemingly overcrowded living room, as well as the two chairs and monster television set. The sucker had to be at least six feet across. As she tried to plan a layout, more things were brought into the home. She looked at Lucy when she said her name.

"I haven't any idea what I'm doing." Lucy said she looked it. "I mean, he bought this stuff before he knew me. All of it to redo his house, so I'm not sure what his plan is."

"You could ask him." Allie told her that he was in a meeting. "Yes, I heard. So, what would you do with it if it was yours to do with?"

"I'd get rid of these chairs, first of all." They were old and probably broken, plus they didn't match anything that he'd gotten. There were tears on the upholstery, and she could see that one of the arms was loose on the bigger of the two. "Then these lamps. I'm thinking since he got the same amount that was in here in the first place, he meant to replace these. But some of them are really old and pretty. Should we just toss them out?"

"No. There's a person in town that deals with some of this sort of thing. You know, helping out people that otherwise might not have things. I'd say have him come out, see what he can use, and trash the rest." Allie nodded. "As for these new couches, they're lovely, aren't they? I wonder how much he paid for them?"

Allie had no idea, and the next time someone came in with yet another box, she asked them to take something that was going out to the barn. That way it wouldn't get damp should the weather turn. Within an hour, with the help of Lucy, she had the room set up, as well as the dining room table and chairs ready to be used. She only hoped that it was marginally what Christian had wanted.

"Christian said that he'd be home by dinner, that we should go ahead and order something. Or I can start something here and have him pick up some steaks to have. Which do you prefer?" Allie said she didn't care which; in actuality, she was too tired to even think of food and told Lucy that. "Well, you have been very busy today. Let me take care of dinner and you have a nice lie down on the sofa. The rest of them are cutting down the boxes that were brought in, as well as getting the grill and furniture for the deck put together. It's a lovely night for a cookout, and we'll have some fun too."

"I don't want to have to leave this all to you." Lucy told her that there wasn't anything left to do other than to have the grill lit when the time came. Yawning again, Allie told her that she would lie down, but to wake her when Christian returned. "It won't be long, but I am really tired."

"You go on ahead, Allie. There isn't anything here we can't take care of." Nodding, she found herself not only on the sofa, but covered up and with a nice pillow too. Closing her eyes, she felt her body just fall overboard into sleep.

Waking to someone touching her cheek, she looked up into the most incredibly beautiful face she had ever seen. When she smiled at Christian, he leaned down and kissed her. It was soft, wonderfully sexy, and above all, very much needed.

"I have to tell you something." He kissed her again, then deepened it the third time. "Christ, I could do that all day. But I wanted to tell you that I'm in love with you. I only just figured it out."

"You are?" He nodded, leaned closer to her ear, and bit her. Allie felt her entire body sizzle and pop. "You do that very nicely. I don't think anyone has kissed me like that before."

"You're making me crazy with need." She laughed and sat up when he did. "Food is here. And as much as I'd like to stay here and finish this, I don't think that my parents would enjoy hearing me make you scream."

"Would you? I mean, I've not had a lot of good experiences when it comes to sex. I mean.... Even before Park, it wasn't all that good." He told her that it would be with him. "You're awfully sure of yourself. What makes you think you'll have any better luck than anyone else did?"

He stood up and pulled her to his body. Once there, she could not only feel his erection, but also his need, like it was a blanket wrapped around them both. And when he lifted her face up to look into her eyes, she could see it there. He really did love her.

"We should go. If we go now, I won't have to be in trouble for taking you to our bedroom and having wild and passionate sex with you while my family holds dinner for us, for the next several years." She nodded, but neither of them moved. "Christ."

51

The kiss was breathtaking. He kissed her like he was ready to have her for dinner rather than whatever was going to be served on the table. And when he pulled her body to his, his hands cupping her ass and bringing her closer to his cock, she pulled away and threw back her head.

The bite along her throat startled her. And when he kissed the hurt, she pulled his head from her neck and kissed him. It was all she could do not to come when he rocked her over his hardness.

"Come for me. I want to taste you while you have your pleasure." She shook her head, telling him that she'd never come before. "Trust me, you will when I press you against that wall behind you. Come for me, Allie. I'll bite you and bring you harder for it."

She moaned when he took a step. The movement of his legs, the way his cock seemed to be pressing against her clit over and over, had her hanging on. And when her body hit the wall behind her, it was as if a switch had been flipped and she came hard.

His hands held her still while he rocked into her body. She thought of his cock, thick as it slid in and out of her. Allie's body responded to her imagination, the visual of the two of them as they were entangled in the sheets of their bed. His hands, darker than hers, touched her in places that were hot with need. And when he told her to come, his whisper in her ear might well have been a scream to her. Allie felt her body rear up and climax like it had been made especially for this.

"Again." She wasn't sure that she could, but her mind and body had different plans and came as he had commanded. His mouth covered hers when she started to scream, and Allie found that to be all the more fulfilling when he seemed to swallow her release.

When he backed from the wall, she held tightly onto his shoulders. Neither of them spoke. Allie wasn't even sure what she would say to him. As he held her, she tried to get her heartrate under control and her breathing to not be so harsh. Looking at her when he lifted her chin up, he smiled.

"I'm going to be very painfully aware of you until my family is gone." She started to ask him what he meant when he rocked into her. "I don't think I've ever been this hard in my life. And the thought of spilling myself into you has my head spinning."

"We can tell them to go home." He sighed heavily and put her down on the floor. "You're going to make me go in there, aren't you? After treating me to the best climax I've ever had."

He kissed her quickly on the mouth and took two long steps back. "It will only get better from here. This I promise you."

She believed him. As he pulled her by her hand to the dining room, all she could think about was that she did. Not just on this, but everything that came from his lips. The promises that he made to her about being safe with him. His faith that they would be good together. Even that when they went to bed — and there was no doubt that they would — it would be so good between them that there would be nothing to come between them.

~~~

Denny watched his sons. Mostly, he kept an eye on Christian, but he looked at Brayden too. Both of them were in over their heads with their mates and he was tickled about it. When his own lovely mate touched her fingers to his arm, he looked at her.

"They're going to be fine now. But I have to worry about

something. His cat seems to be right on the edge all the time. Have you noticed that?" He said that he had, a lot more since Allie had joined them. "Why is that? Brayden is so calm around others that touch Dane, but Christian is like a wild animal when the others are too close."

"I don't know. I have a feeling that he doesn't either. It seems to bother him on levels that upset him too." Lucy said she had noticed he fought with himself much more too. "I'll have to do some asking around. Could be that he's new to all this, but I don't know."

"I know they love each other. It's with every touch they have between them." He smiled as Dane smacked Brayden's hand when he touched her when she was mad at him. "You think the rest of them will be finding their other halves soon? I'm telling you, Lucy, I'm looking for one of them to tell me that they're going to have us a grandchild. After being alone here, with just our sons, I'd love to have us a little granddaughter to come over."

"I was thinking the same thing just this morning when I was baking cookies for the sale at the library. How much fun would it have been to have a granddaughter helping out?" Denny took her hand in his as they listened to their growing family talk. "Christmas is in a few weeks. Perhaps we should hedge our bets and buy each of them a little baby gift. Just to push them along into our way of thinking."

"Won't work with Christian. You know that as well as I do. And I'd be terrified that Dane would come back on us and make us use it. I don't think I'm suited to sleep in a small cradle." They both laughed and the boys turned to look at them. Denny told them to go on with whatever they were doing and he looked at Lucy. "But, I do think we can have some fun with this. How about we go ahead and get them each a nice rocker? And maybe clean out some of their things from the attic. I know for a fact that we have the baby bed from Brayden. Might be out of date, but we can just pass it along."

"I think that's a brilliant idea. And I can get to knitting again. I so loved making them sweaters when they were younger." Denny was warming to the idea, and began a checklist of things that he wanted to work on as well.

There was a swing set that was for sale at the local hardware store. He might just have someone come out and put it up for him. And then there was the pool they'd had put in a few years back. No one was using it so they'd not filled it. But he thought they might want to now. After putting a large fence around it.

By the time dinner was over and the dishes cleaned up, he wanted to get home and take care of a couple more things that he'd thought of. He might have been pushing it a little, but he didn't care right now. He had two sons with mates, and no word on them having children yet. As he drove himself and Lucy home, he was thinking hard on things when he realized there was a car in his drive. One that he didn't know.

"You stay here." She nodded when he said he'd see who it was. "Call the boys in for me. I'm a might nervous, and I don't want them coming here with guns blazing for no reason. I've yet to replenish the clinic, and I don't have bandages."

"You just be careful." He said that he would as he opened the door and started out of his car. "Denny, you get hurt and I'm going to beat you senseless. I swear that I will."

He kissed her on the mouth and got out of the car. Closing the door brought the man sitting on his porch to his feet, and someone around the house too. He didn't say anything, but watched the two of them. It wasn't until he heard his sons telling him that they were on their way that he felt a little better.

"Hello." Denny nodded, but didn't move closer when the man stepped off his porch. "I've come to have a conversation with your son, the attorney."

"He doesn't live here." The man nodded. "Who are you, and what do you think to accomplish by being where you weren't invited?"

"My name? Well now, I'd be wrong in giving you that, don't you think?" He pulled out his gun and pointed it at him. Denny heard the door to his car open, but didn't turn to see what was going on. "Now, here is what you're going to do for us. I'd like for you to invite us in, and then we'll have a nice conversation. That way, your wife won't get hurt."

"You harm her and you're going to regret that." Lucy stood beside him, but she wasn't alone. A thug held her there with a gun to her head. Denny felt his cat shimmer over his skin. "You all right, love?"

"Yes, but that brute broke my purse, and it was my favorite too." He asked her again, through their link, if she was all right. *Yes. I didn't fight him. The gun was too close, and I think he wanted me to try something. Oh, Denny, what are we going to do?*

For now, anything but go into that house. I don't think we'd survive if they got us there. He looked at the man when he spoke. "What do you want? And I'm not inviting you into my home. So, you tell me what it is you're doing here so I can tell you no and get on with our lives."

"I want to speak to your son, Christian." Denny saw three of his sons coming around the side of the house. They were in cat form, and he was so relieved that he nearly staggered under his profound relief. "And as soon as he cooperates, we'll all live to see another day."

"What do you think you're going to force me to do?" Denny watched Christian as he came from the other side of the house. The man turned when Christian spoke again, but didn't take his gun off Denny. "By the way, you should know that the other four men you had out in the field are all dead. It's not very sporting of you to try and ambush my family."

"Mr. Stanton, just the man I've been looking for. I'm here to ask you politely to come back with me to the city and talk to the judge on the case for Mr. Davis. It would save us all a great deal of time if you came along nicely. If not...well, I don't really care what your feelings on this are. You'll do as we wish either way." Denny watched two more men coming from the same direction Christian had. He thought they were the bad guys, but then realized they were police officers. "Now, as I was telling your lovely and for now, living parents here, I need to have a conversation with you."

"You're talking. I'm listening. Sounds like we're having a conversation. Who sent you? Joy or Park? Wait, can't be Park. He had his privileges taken from him today. It seems that he made some demands of the wrong person while incarcerated, and got himself put in a nice lonely cell." Denny saw Christian smile, and knew that whatever he said next was not going to bode well for the men that had invaded his property. "Must be Joy Hartman. How is it she said she was going to pay you off? Insurance? Well, there isn't any. Not with her as the benefactor, nor her son. Money? She doesn't have a pot to piss in. Sex? Nasty, but if that is worth a prison sentence for you, then by all means, you go ahead and try to force my hand. But I'd be careful if I were you. My family, in case you didn't know, they have some very powerful teeth."

"Teeth? What the hell are you going on about? Not that

it matters much to me. But yes, I'll tell you that Joy sent me. She asked me to see about talking you into changing your mind. As for the payment, if there was one that was going to exchange hands, that is none of your business." Christian nodded, then looked at Denny before the man continued. "Come on now. Leaving with me could save a lot of time and effort. And you really don't want your parents hurt, do you?"

"Are you all right? Mom? Dad?" He nodded, and Lucy told him she was going to be better when she had some grandchildren. "Yes, well, if it's all the same to you, for the moment anyway, I'll take care of this first. I mean, I'd hate to think that men like Randal James would just show up anytime he wanted to."

"All right. But you'll work on that, won't you, son?" Christian nodded and looked back at Randal. "Christian, be careful, please?"

"I plan on it." Christian laughed again as he walked toward Randal. "You see, Mom, I've been very smart my whole life, and never take chances unless I have no choice in the matter. Like today. My hand was forced and I had to call in some extra help. Randal? I'd like for you to meet my brothers."

The low growl had Randal turning, but he didn't drop the gun. Brayden was a big cat, all of them were, but he walked right up to the man and didn't just knock his gun out of his hand, but pushed him to his butt too. The others came around the side of the house as well, and Julian and Wyatt stood next to him. The man holding Denny and Lucy backed away after dropping his weapon. Denny pulled Lucy into his arms just as a falcon landed in the yard in front of them all. Dane shifted, holding her own gun and wearing a huge smile.

"Hello there, Randal. It's been a long time." Randal

whimpered, and Denny wondered what she'd done to him before. "You should have been warned this was my family. I'm going to have to make some calls on your behalf now. Why don't I give you a sheet of paper and you can write down your next of kin? That'll save me some time after I kill you."

"Dane, no one told me you were related to these men." She shrugged, moving closer to Randal as she put her gun away. "Does Mr. Sams have to know about this?"

"Oh yes. In fact, he already does." Denny watched all the men, but mostly he kept an eye on Randal. The man was terrified of his daughter-in-law, and he loved it. "You should know better than to take on a family member, Randal. That is going to cost you big time."

"I didn't do anything but push around a few threats." She nodded just as the men from the side of the house came out. "You called in the Feds? Mother fuck, Dane. What do you think Mr. Sams is going to say about that? You fucked up big time. If you let me go, I'll never tell him what you've done."

"No deal. And he knows. He's wiped his hands of you, so to speak." The two men picked Randal up and cuffed him. As he was being dragged away, Brayden's big cat stood by Dane, and Denny had a moment to wonder where Allie was. When she joined Dane, he wondered about that as well.

The Feds took away Randal, but that still left the police to deal with. The other four men, ones he had thought were dead, were taken away as well, and the police were left to do clean up. And there wasn't much of that left to do either. Surprisingly, they didn't grumble about it once. Apparently, Randal was a big deal for a lot of people, and the locals were glad to turn him over without any involvement.

"I'd like a word with you, if you don't mind, Mr. Stanton." Denny nodded at the man in front of him. "It's about this leap.

I wanted to know who I talk to in order to work for Dane. She's the stuff legends are made of."

"I think so as well, but I'd not mention that when you talk to her. And as far as I know, she'd be the one that you'd have to talk to. I tend to stay out of that business." Roger Dent, the man who had asked, introduced himself to him and Lucy. "You boys, you were close enough to come running when necessary. I'm assuming that we'll be seeing a lot of strangers in town for now?"

"More than you think have been here for some time. Not anything to do with your family, mind you, but this is a nice town and a good place to go when they're off duty." Denny loved his hometown. "My wife and I, we've purchased the Cody house and farm."

He knew the farm. It had been empty for some time, but he didn't remember if it was just that the family had passed on or taxes. That was getting a lot of the land around here, it seemed.

When Roger moved away, he stood where he was and watched. This was going to be an issue, he thought, for as long as Christian didn't jump when that woman, Joy, told him to. Smiling to himself, Denny wondered how long it would be before it all came crashing down on the woman's head. And he had no doubt that it would.

The police did a sweep of the yard and the house before he and Lucy were allowed to go inside. He was glad for it. No telling what those idiots had done to his home.

Chapter 5

"I thought it best that they didn't associate her with Christian just yet." Allie wasn't sure that worked, but as Dane explained the reasons for things, she thought about what she'd seen today. They'd all converged at Christian's home, to let the police and whatever other people have a look around. "There will be others coming, I think, so the only way that I could think that they'd not use her against Christian was to take her out of the picture for now. They'll figure it out soon enough, but right now, we have an advantage."

The men that had gone to Christian's parents' house had been people sent to force Christian into doing something he couldn't or wouldn't do. She wasn't sure what they would have done had she been around...perhaps killed her to make sure that he did it. At the very least, they would have hurt her. She looked at Christian when he sat beside her.

"You need to convert me." He kissed the back of her hand. "Today, if it's possible. I won't be able to survive them should they come for me, and we both know that they'll be back. Someone might get hurt then."

"All right." She expected some resistance, but was glad there wasn't. "As soon as we finish up what we started at the house, we'll do it."

Sex. Or making love. They had been in his room when the call had come out that his parents had visitors. He'd not wanted to go until he realized, through information from Dane, that they were sent to kidnap Denny to make Christian take the trial.

"Will those men go to jail?" Dane told her that they were being taken care of. "I don't understand that. You mean that the guy you threatened him with—Sams, I think his name was—he'll be taking care of it? I don't think that's good, do you?"

"Yes. And no, Walter isn't taking care of them, but the Feds are. They're being offered a very good deal to turn on Joy or Park, whichever one hired them." Allie told him that Joy had done it. Then she asked Dane how Park could have done it if it had been him. "He's very resourceful and knows a lot of people that would do just about anything, even to their own mother, to be able to get some ready cash. But as you said, it was Joy. That's a lot of baggage she picked up on this. And soon she'll get caught and taken into custody as well."

The room was talking in general. She wasn't really paying attention, but when Colton asked how things were going to get paid for, like hitmen, she listened to them. Colton asked his question again.

"I didn't know that Park still had any money. Does he have a stash that we don't know about?" They all looked at Christian. "You had a meeting with Mr. Hartman. He...Park is no longer getting anything."

Christian shook his head and explained. "No, he's not. Nor is his mom. They've both been written out of the will, and Landon has filed for divorce from Joy. She's in jail too, but due to be released the day after tomorrow from the episode at the mall. This other, hiring the men to do this to me, she'll get hit with that later when they have more evidence. It'll be up to the arresting officer on how long they'll wait to take her in again." Allie thought about the woman and her being out to do damage. There wasn't any doubt in her mind that she would, too. She thought of ways to make her think he was working for them. Christian turned to her. "What is it you're thinking? You have an idea?"

"I do, but it's sort of farfetched. And doubtful you'll like it." Christian told her to share it. "I believe you should wait until she goes and sees her son again. She'll be surrounded by a bunch of cops, and we all know how she hates to be arrested."

No one moved. Nor did any of them tell her that was a stupid idea. It wasn't until Levi started laughing that she frowned at them. Everyone was either thinking it was a great idea, or they thought she was insane and were humoring her.

"You do have that right. Williams is still recovering from his little spat with her. And he isn't a small man. If just having her papers served to her ticked her off that much, you can only imagine how pissy she's going to be when she's arrested for attempted kidnapping. Christ, I love it." Julian looked around the room as he continued. "It's perfect. And will buy us time to get things in a row and off our back while he works on things for his case against her. This way, she might even screw up more."

"She usually sees him daily. Picking a day when she's off guard will give us an advantage. I like this idea as well." She felt embarrassed then, but Christian turned to her and smiled. "Thank you for this. You might have saved us a little more time in getting our ducks in a row." Christian started pacing as he talked it through. "I'd have to speak to Landon. I don't think he'd have an issue with it, being that he's divorcing his wife and cut them both out, but he'll need to know what she's been up to. And that she'll be arrested soon. I can call him in a bit. After we have a few things figured out."

"So, you think it'll work?" He said he didn't know why not. "Well, if either of them find out, it could be bad for a lot of people. I mean, that guy that came here, he could be just a drop in the bucket for the amount of people that either of them could have hired. Maybe, while you talk to him about it, you should ask Landon if he could, I don't know, put something out there that says that they've been cut out."

"I'll ask him." Christian kissed her hard and fast on her mouth. "You're brilliant. I don't even want to know how you came up with this idea, but I'm loving it. It has some things that could go wrong, but with Joy in jail and no reason to think her son will get out legally, then I think we'll all be safe too."

Her cell phone was ringing when she got up to go to the kitchen. They'd hired a cook. Well, someone had. Mrs. Apple came with great recommendations, and she liked her. Allie was going to see about getting some snacks fixed for everyone, and pulled out her phone just as she entered the big room.

"Darling? Is that you?" She had to look at the phone number to see if she knew the person on the other end. "It's Mom. We had to get new phones, and I was calling to give you the number. Heath has it in his head that you won't answer if you don't know who it is. I told him you would know it was us. Honey, what's that number again?"

Sitting down at the big butcher block, she looked up when

Mrs. Apple set a glass of tea in front of her. She had no idea how she might look to the older woman, but she left her there to no doubt get Christian.

"Mom? Where are you? I thought you and Dad weren't coming home until Christmas." Her mother laughed...she had the strangest sense of humor. "Mom?"

"Yes, we're coming home, but you do realize that Christmas is in six weeks. Why, next week is Thanksgiving." To be honest, she'd forgotten about either holiday. "Dad and I were wondering if you could clear it with your landlord to have us park in your lot there for a week or two. We'll live in it, so there is no reason for you to be put out. But maybe it'd be nice to have a hot shower that wasn't timed for a change. You know your dad and keeping the water at a certain level."

She looked at Christian when he entered the room. Asking her mom to hold on, she watched as Christian showed her how to put the phone on mute. Allie told him what her mom had said.

"Would you object to inviting them here? I mean, we have plenty of room, and they might enjoy having a real house for a change. They could use as much water as they wanted." Her parents here? For the holidays? She wasn't sure and said as much to Christian. "It'll be just fine. Do they have much in the way of contact with shifters and such?"

"Yes. Dad used to work for one a long time ago, and Mom's best friend is a wolf. But to stay here. Do you know...? Well, you don't know. My parents are nice, but strange. I mean, like they're considered weird by most people." Christian kissed her on the forehead and went to the refrigerator. "Besides, I don't know how they'd react to me living here."

"Then when they arrive, we'll have a wedding. Did you want anything to drink? I'm having a sandwich. And I think that your brother should stay as well. I like Perry." She stared at him and he smiled again. "I can hear your mom calling your name. Find out when they'll arrive, and we'll see about getting you converted before they get here."

Her mom was indeed talking. Not to her, but to her dad. Something about the timer and how she'd messed him up. While she listened to them, she thought of them staying here. It would be good to see them again, but for how long? The next six weeks? Christian took the phone from her and fixed it so he could speak, but he said her mom's name twice before he smiled.

"This is Christian Stanton. Allie and I are getting married." The squeal from her mom had him jerking the phone away for a few seconds. "Yes, I'm very sure. She and I will hold off on getting married if you think you guys would like to come and stay with us for a while. We have plenty of room."

Her mom spoke and she waited for Christian to hand her back the phone. But the longer they spoke, the more she realized it would be wonderful having them here. Lucy entered the room with them and Allie told her what was going on.

"Oh, how lovely. I was hoping we'd get to meet them." Allie wondered what they were going to say once they did meet them. "We should plan a large welcome party. Perhaps even turn it into a wedding." She told her that was what Christian had said too. "I knew he was a smart boy the moment I had him."

Christian handed her the phone and she put it to her ear just as he told his mom that was an excellent idea. As they planned behind her, she listened to her mom telling her that she was so happy for her.

"He's a wonderful man, isn't he, dear? I want you to be

happy." She said that she was. "Well, that's so wonderful. And a lawyer too. My goodness, I'm so happy for my little girl. I don't suppose you could talk Perry into coming by once or twice while we visit, can you? I miss him as well." She told her mom that Perry was out of town right now, but would be back in a few days. "Good. It's been a while since we've all been together. And now you're getting married. My goodness, where has all the time gone?"

They talked for a little while longer. Allie moved out into the sunroom, a place that was starting to fill up with not just plants that would fill the house year-round, but also the beginning of a great many herbs that would be planted in the spring. As she played with the leaves on the basil plant, she listened to her parents talk to each other more than her.

"Your father wants me to make sure you want him there. What with him being in a wheelchair and all." She said of course she did. "I don't want to put you out, dear. But I must say that it is exciting to be in a place that doesn't move every time you take a step. And to have a shower in a bathroom sounds heavenly."

"Maybe when you get here, you'll want to settle down again. Have a house. Christian and I would love to have you around when we have kids." She didn't say anything. "Mom, I have money and so does Christian. If you want, we can help you buy you a home. I don't mind at all."

"I don't know, Allie. It's been so long since we've had roots." Her mom lowered her voice. "I think your dad is tired of this as well. I have to do most of the setting up, and I think he feels inadequate in that. We don't need anything big, just a couple of rooms and a little bitty yard."

Allie smiled. So, they had been thinking of it. That made her both excited and afraid. Excited to have them around again, and afraid that they'd not enjoy it. Her parents weren't picky, but they were a little odd when it came to their own life. She loved them dearly, but knew that they would go or stay, and it would matter little what she wanted.

"I'll look around. There's no hurry for you to find something. Like Christian said, there is plenty of room here." When she hung up after assuring her that they'd be welcome and that she'd call Perry, Allie wandered back into the living room.

She'd not realized how long she had been gone when she found the big room empty. Going in search of Christian to tell him she was sorry, Allie found him in the big office on the phone. Landon had called.

~~~

"I can do that for you. I understand completely, Landon. You don't have to tell me again that you're sorry. We're all fine, and so are you." Landon told him between sobbing that he'd never thought they'd hurt his family. "I think it would be best if you stayed right where you are. That way, we don't have to worry about you either."

"Are you going to go see her? Before she's released?" Landon wanted her and Park to know that they were no longer a part of his estate. "You think that will make them back off? From your family, at least?"

"I don't think so, but yes, I'll go and see them in the morning. Anything else you need done?" He watched Allie circle the room, touching this and that. Making sure it was put back when she picked something up. Landon told him that he'd had the locks changed already, and Christian had patrols roaming the grounds. "The staff is aware of the changes as well, and have been told to call the police if they should come there. Even your butler told me that he hoped one of them did come by. He had a few things to say to them."

"Yes, Burt never did like either of them. I didn't know about Park when I asked Joy to marry me. Well, she said she had a kid, and it never occurred to me to check it out. I think.... Well, loneliness can make a person do the strangest things." He knew that. Lashing out at Allie the first time he saw her had proven that. "I'm going to let you go. I'm sure you have plenty to do other than talk to an old man who should have known better."

"Don't worry about it, Landon. Anytime you need to talk, you call me. Or even Allie. She'd love to help you out as well." Allie smiled and nodded at him. "She's healing well, and after this week, she'll be my cougar. And her parents are coming to stay for a little while."

After a little more conversation, he hung up. Christian didn't move but watched her glide around the room, as if she was stalling. He let her, thinking that she needed this more than he did her. At least he thought so.

"I hope you don't mind, but I offered to help my parents buy a home here. I don't know that they will, but I did volunteer us to help out." He told her that was fine by him, making a mental note to find them something and purchase it as she continued. "I believe I told you that my dad is in a wheelchair."

"You did. You said that your dad was in a horrific accident at work and lost both legs." She nodded as she sat down on the chair across from him. "Did they get a settlement?"

"No. They had this shark of a lawyer come by the house and take all kinds of notes, but he didn't pursue it. Something about him getting a partnership and not having time to go after them." He asked her how long it had been. "Five years ago, next summer. For a while there, it was touch and go on whether or not he'd be able to do anything on his own. But I think I get my stubbornness from my father. When you tell him he can't do something, he will just because you said he couldn't. Are we going to have sex?"

"No. We're going to make love. I love you. Sex is just for people who have an itch to take care of. I want to make love with you." She nodded; he could tell she was distracted. "Want to tell me what's wrong?"

"I don't know anything about you. I mean, I know what I've heard. Nothing personal. Not that it's necessary, but I don't want to feel like we're going to hate one another after we have sex...make love." He asked her to come to sit on his lap. "You just want to jump my bones."

"I do, but I think you're right. We know very little about each other." She came to him and sat on his lap. He held her against his chest and thought of things that he'd like her to know. "I've been a lawyer, I think, my entire life. It's all I ever wanted to do, to make sure that justice is served for someone and to uphold the law. It doesn't always work out that way, but I do give it my best."

"I was a social worker before Park. I helped as best I could, but I realized early on that it wasn't for me. I thought that I was going to save all the children of the world and make sure that they were safe. I was losing more than I was saving on a daily basis. Mostly I was able to put a Band-Aid on things but never fix it. I felt like a failure." She looked at him. "I know that we both want children, but I'd like to be able to help some as well. We don't have to adopt them if you don't want, but I would like to give some a boost up when we can."

"I agree with you, and we can adopt too. The idea of helping them might make the world a better place for a few." She nodded and laid her head back on his shoulder. "I love the holidays. More so now that we're all home for good. I think you knew this, but Brayden traveled a great deal before he found Dane. She works for some people that some think are bad guys, but I think she doesn't care. I'm the second child of my parents, as you know, and I have a doctorate, just as the rest of us do. In my field, I'm Doctor Stanton in title only. As are the rest of my family."

"You're all so accomplished. I didn't want to be a corporate person. I ended up in the corporate world when I worked for the state, but nothing since. I like being in business on my own." He told her that he did as well. "I need a job. I don't know what I'll do, maybe continue to teach self-defense or just find something else, but I need one. For me."

She turned then, so that her legs were on either side of his. Holding her back, she adjusted herself so that she was riding over his cock. He looked at her face and saw love, compassion, as well as a little fear.

"What is it you want from me?" She stared at him and he kissed her gently on the mouth. "I can take you right here or upstairs in our room."

"Both." He nodded. The way he was feeling, Christian thought he could take her several times without missing a beat. "I don't want you to be dissatisfied in me. While I've had sex, before everything with he who should not be named, I wasn't ever any good at it."

"I could never be dissatisfied in you. I love you. There will never be anything you do that will disappoint me." He rocked upward as he watched her face. "You're beautiful. I want to see all of you, feast on you as well."

He took her blouse off, unbuttoning each of the buttons slowly and kissing the skin as he exposed it. Allie rode him now, her body swaying over his cock back and forth while he

71

made short work of her bra too.

"The way you touch me, it's like you're heating me up. Not just my girly parts, but all of me." He told her that he was going to get to her girly parts too. "I hope so. The anticipation is killing me."

"My cock is burning to be inside of you. And my cat...I hope you don't mind, but he wants his fill of you too. Drinking from your pussy while you come." Allie stopped him from taking her breast into his mouth. "You don't want that? I can understand. It's—"

"Do it. Now. I want to feel him touching me with his tongue." He sat her on his desk, pushing things to the floor as he went. Taking off her pants and underwear, he opened her legs wide and looked at her drenched in her cream. "Please. You have to do something. I'm aching right now."

Leaning down to her, he licked her from gate to clit. Then taking the small treat into his mouth, he suckled at it until she cried out, her body quivering with her release. Taking off his shirt and pants, he let his cat take him.

His cat didn't hesitate, but put his large paws on her thighs and dove into her pussy. Her screams, each release from her, were bountiful and loud. Allie begged for more, told him with words and her body that she was enjoying herself. Then she pulled him up from her.

"Take me. Please. I need to feel you filling me." He took his body back, his cock straining hard. "Please. Now, Christian, now."

Slamming into her—there was no hope for him being gentle now—he cried out when she strangled him with her sheath. As he fucked her, taking his time while she laid on his desk, his hand opened her knees for him to watch.

Every time his cock would leave her body, he could see

himself bathed in her cream. Slick with her need, he slid in and out of her quickly, feeling her small tremors with each movement. And when she screamed, louder than she had before, Christian felt his own climax race over him, from the top of his head to the bottom of his feet. And when he was empty, his body reeling with it, he stepped back and his cat took him again. It was time. She needed to be converted, and his cat seemed to know that.

The first bite was the hardest, to her belly and deep inside to tear into her intestine to start the long process. The cat tore at her tender flesh, making the change now necessary to save her life. She didn't cry, didn't beg him to stop as he held the bite while his saliva worked to heal and change her.

The second bite was to her left arm. She held him to her while he did that, kept telling him in whispered words, that she loved him for this. That no matter what happened, she would love him forever. The third and final bite was to her thigh. Christian heard bones snap as he tore her flesh, and knew that should she not make it that he'd take his own life now. He loved her that much.

Almost within minutes he felt the difference in her taste. Allie's heart rate was picking up now, almost within normal ranges for a cat. Moaning when he let her go, Christian shifted, taking his body back, and pulled on his pants.

Taking her to their bathroom, he stood with her under the spray of water to clean them both up. He didn't try to wash her, just let the warm water rinse away any sweat she had as well as blood. There had been a great deal of it, but he'd known, from others changing mates, that there would be. Drying her was a challenge, but soon he had her tucked into their bed and he laid down beside her.

Christian thought about letting his family know what

he'd done, but didn't want to talk to anyone right now. It hurt him, on so many levels, to have caused her pain. But he was glad now that he'd done it. That she was his mate in all ways.

He told her of his plans for when she woke. "We'll find your mom and dad a house. And even if they don't live in it full time, they'll have it to come home to. Also, we'll need to set you up with an office. Perry is going to be traveling a great deal now, and you need a place to help others."

He talked to her until the sunlight filled the room. Then, pulling a light blanket over them, he fell asleep, knowing that from now on, they'd be one.

Chapter 6

"I don't think you're listening to me, Joy. He's filed for and gotten a divorce, and he's put out an order stating that neither you nor your son can have access to his house or any of his accounts." Joy nodded at the man and asked him where the new keys were. "I'm sure that I don't know. Perhaps he took them with him. But he's not going to allow you entrance to his home."

"Then where am I supposed to live? On the streets? I don't think so. Just give me the keys and I'll go home. We can work this out. But not while he's gone." She wasn't sure that the man was listening to her. The problem was, she was worried that Landon had really done it this time, locked her out of her lovely life. "Call him. Tell him that I'm not happy and he'll be on the next plane back. He has taken the plane, right?"

"I don't know where he is. Nor, if I knew, would I tell you. He's not going to be coming back here to allow you to come into his home." She pointed out that it was her home. "No, not according to the deed. It's never been yours. Nothing is. And since you signed the agreement when you were married, you don't get anything after the divorce either. You should have thought of these things when you were living with him. Now, it's much too late for you to consider asking him for money."

"Landon didn't mean for me not to get anything. I'm sure that's a mistake on your part. And there's something going on with my credit cards as well. I was arrested the other day when that dumb bitch told me that it had been declined and she cut it up." She could still see the glee on the woman's face as she did that. "I can't be without money, James. That's just not right. Landon and I had an agreement. A verbal agreement that he'd never take away my credit cards."

Not true. In fact, for the last month he'd been telling her almost daily that she was overspending and was going to get cut off. Joy didn't believe him, of course. Not even when Park, her baby boy's cards stopped working. Now there was a person who overspent. But she didn't. Only bought what she wanted, not things that struck her fancy one day and was tossed out the next. She sold off what she didn't need anymore, unlike her son.

"I don't know what to tell you, Joy. What's done is done, and there is nothing you or anyone can do about it. He's a man with a lot of money and pull. And it's all done legally. Mr. Stanton didn't make any mistakes...not that he ever does, but—"

"What do you mean, Mr. Stanton? Christian stopped working for the family. I couldn't even get him to take the fraudulent case that is against my son. He can't have anything to do with this as he's not our attorney any longer." James pointed out that he wasn't her attorney, but he was still Landon's. "Then that makes him mine as well. We're a family, and that means what is his is mine and what's mine is his.

I want you to call Stanton and tell him that the case is still ready for him to take care of. My son is in jail, going to prison for a crime that he didn't commit. And don't you dare tell me again that Christian doesn't work for me. He does, because I'm still married to Landon until I say so."

She was getting it...as much as she was frustrating him, she was equally frustrated. Joy understood that Landon had filed for divorce. That he had locked them out of everything, including the accounts. She also understood why he'd done it. He was pissed off at her and Park because of all the trouble they'd caused him lately. Yes, she understood that. But that wasn't any reason for her to be without. Not one bit.

"I'm not going to call anyone. Nor am I going to make demands on a man that I know for a fact does not work for you. You, as I have pointed out before, should have made plans for something like this. And since you didn't, I'm afraid that you're out of luck." He stood up then and pointed to the door. "I think it's well past time that you left, Joy. We're done here unless you can afford to pay me, otherwise you'll have to find someone else to represent you."

Leaving the attorney's office a short while later, having not gotten any keys or an advance on the now useless credit cards, she pulled out her cell phone to try to call Landon again. He was avoiding her, that was all, and once she could talk to him, the sooner they could get this mess cleaned up. Besides, nothing was working out the way she wanted until he was home. There were matters going on that he needed to be around to take care of. And with him gone and no one knowing where, she couldn't get her shit fixed either.

Benson White, such a stupid name, was going to get rid of her husband for her. She'd shown him the insurance policy that Landon had taken out on them both, how much the payoff was, as well as the will. She was sure that the will might have been changed already—Landon would get right on that—but the policy had been her idea, and she was glad when he agreed to take it out on himself. And if he was murdered, she'd get double the ten million he'd had on it. It was her ticket for a better life with her son.

"Hello, Joy. Where's the job located that you wanted me to take care of for you? You've been very helpful up until now, and I can't get paid until the job is finished. Can't finish the job without the whereabouts. What's up?" She told him Landon had left town on a business trip. "Really? What timing for him. What do you say the two of us get together and...go over things again?"

Her body heated up at the thought of his body anywhere near hers again. "I'd like that. But let's go someplace nice. A lovely hotel. The house is being cleaned from top to bottom."

Joy was afraid that if he found out that she'd been locked out, he'd cancel the arrangements that she had with him. And damn it, she wanted Landon dead. It would solve so many problems, like making her flush again. Putting her back in control too. And her son released. She was going to be in huge trouble if she didn't get some income soon.

Like the first time she'd used this ruse to get her son out, she had dangled the policy as payment. The man was dead, of course...his method of payment had been for him to get the police on him for attempted murder. Lucky for her, he'd been killed before he could tell anyone she'd been involved.

Landon had screwed her. There were no two ways about it. Now he was nowhere she could find him to get things back to the way she liked them. And that he'd pulled Stanton in on this really burned her toast. She'd told him to end all relationships with him when he'd cut her son out of his services. But of course, Landon did what he wanted to do. Damn it all.

Making her way to the jail to see her son was next on her list of things to do. She'd meant to see him this morning, but the limo that she'd hired for the day had said her card wasn't any good. So, she'd had to walk to the bank in town, a good mile of dirty roads, and in her best shoes too. The hotel she was staying at had also left her a message about unpaid bills. This was getting ridiculous.

Lucky for her, the morning she'd left for the courthouse she'd picked up the cash that she'd been hoarding. With Landon being so picky about what she spent, she thought it might be a good idea to hide some. But two thousand dollars certainly didn't go far when you had a lifestyle like hers.

Joy had tricked Landon into marrying her. Or so she'd thought. She'd told him she was alone, lonely, and had money of her own. She wasn't either of those things, and at the time, she'd had nothing but about twenty bucks to her name. The only part he'd not been aware of was Park. Well, he knew that she had a son, but she'd led him to believe they weren't close, when Park was her life. Things had started to fall apart a few months ago, but had come to a head only just recently.

Landon had called her into his office just two weeks prior and tossed a sheath of papers at her. She glanced at them but didn't bother picking them up. They weren't divorce papers, not then, so she didn't care.

"If you have something to say, Landon dear, just say it. I have a hair appointment in an hour, and I have yet to have my nails done." He asked her for who. "I'm sorry. What do you mean? For you, of course."

"Are you sure, Joy? I'm thinking that it's for one of the six men you're sleeping with. Well, fucking anyway." She said

79

nothing, mentally counting how many men she was currently seeing, and could think of three more that he apparently didn't know about. "You do know that this house is loyal to me and only me, don't you? And Burt tells me everything."

"He's a busybody." Landon just leaned back in his chair. "What is this all about? You think you can hold something over me? Well, it won't work. You know as well as I that you have a reputation to uphold, and being fucked over by your wife would destroy that."

"Do you really think you could do that, Joy? I don't, but it's nice to know that you're concerned about me a little anyway. Besides, I'm beginning to think I no longer care about that." She'd not expected him to say that, but waited. "The debt that you had before I asked you to marry me is still out there. I didn't pay it off when they came running to me. You should have waited on us actually saying the vows before telling the collectors you were marrying me and that it would be paid soon. Not that it mattered. They notified me of this an entire week before I asked you to marry me. I told them that it had nothing to do with me. So, you'll be responsible for that. Without using my money."

"Your money? I thought it was our money. Like this is *our* house. It's *our* car and *our* debt." He only shook his head. "Don't be ridiculous, Landon. What if it comes out that I'm in over my ears and you didn't help me? You might claim that you don't care about that, but I can make things very sticky for you and you know it."

"I don't care." She thought maybe he didn't either. "In ten days, I'm going to cut your spending off. You'll have an allowance once a month, and that's all you'll get."

"I'm not ten years old doing chores for some spending money." He smiled at her. "Why are you doing this? Because you think you can outsmart me? It won't work, Landon. I know all about you and where the bodies are buried."

"Speaking of which, I found him." Her feet actually ached, she'd been so afraid after he said that. "Your first husband was murdered by Park, and his body has been exhumed. Once Park gets out of prison for the rape of those women, I plan on giving them that information as well. Then there are the two lovers that you had during your marriage to him. They were willing to sign a report for me, telling me just what they got out of the relationship."

"I don't know what you're talking about. My first husband died of natural causes. No one murdered him. Park was just a little boy anyway, so how could he have done it?" But she did know, and he knew it too. "What does it matter about lovers I had long ago? They mean nothing to me now."

"Don't they? If that were true, which I've come to not believe a single word that flows past your lips, then why are you fucking one of them in my house?" She stood up to leave and he barked at her to sit. "You have ten days. That's all, ten, to get your shit together before I take actions that will land you in the sewer I found you in. And as of now, I'm done with Park. Any trouble he gets into now, it's going to be his mess and only his. Prison is the best place for him if you ask me."

The area in the jail where she saw her son was something she wouldn't wish on anyone. There were plain walls with no art. The glass between then was a nuisance that didn't allow her to hug him, and then there were the cameras everywhere that prohibited them from having a good conversation about anything. She hated that they treated him like this, especially since he'd done nothing wrong.

"Mom." He looked at her like he had something on his mind and it didn't bode well for whoever he was pissed at.

"Why am I still in here? I thought you had it all worked out that I was going to have a trial, get freed, and live like I want to? What the fuck is the holdup?"

"Landon." He quirked a brow at her. "He's got a burr up his ass about everything I do anymore. He's also filed for divorce. And before you ask me, yes, I've tried to talk to him, but he's out of the country or something and I can't find him."

Park laughed, like it was the funniest thing in the world to him. He was lucky at this moment that there was something between them, or she might have hit him with the phone she had to use.

"So, he's gone and done it, has he? Well, I can't say that we didn't see that one coming. What is he doing to compensate you for being married to him for seven years? Alimony is going to be big, I'm betting. I think we can live on that for a time, don't you?" She shook her head. "You can't think you're not going to share, Mother dear. We're both being fucked in the ass by this."

"I signed a prenup." That shut him up. "I never thought that it would come to this, Park. Never. And now that he's cut me off, as well as you, I can't get any ready cash, nor am I allowed back in our home."

"What do you mean, he's cut you off? Are you telling me that in addition to taking away my lifestyle, he's done the same to you? How could he? And why didn't you tell me about the prenup, Mom? What the hell were you thinking? Or were you?" She said that he was mad about a few things he'd found out about. "Like what? You mean anything to do with me?"

Joy nodded, but didn't speak. The recordings could get them all in deep shit right now. Instead, she watched his face until he got it. It took him longer to sort through what people

82

considered his bad deeds than she thought it would, but when he paled, she continued. Park was just experimenting with life and the things that it offered. Didn't they see that?

"He told me some things right after you were arrested. Then he filed for divorce and shut me out of everything and then left. The plane is gone. No one will help me find him, and I haven't any idea how much longer I can stay in the hotel without them kicking me out. This is not the way I wanted to spend my life, Park. I need you here to take care of me." He snorted at her. "What am I supposed to do? I can't live like white trash, Park. I'm not built for that."

"I haven't any idea. But since you can't seem to get your shit together, you've fucked me over as well. Damn it all to fuck and back. I don't want to be in here any longer, Mom. How are you going to make sure I get a good trial and freed?" She watched him talk to someone in the room with him. He was polite to them, which meant they were either bigger or one of the guards. "I only have four minutes left, so I want you to write this down."

She got out the pad of paper she carried with her all the time now. Things in her head would be gone when she saw a pretty bauble or lovely dress. Writing down the store where she'd seen it as well as the numbers on it had saved her a lot of time when she needed something new and could sneak it into the house.

"I need some cash. I don't have anything in my account as of now. See to that for me." She just looked at him and wondered where he thought she was going to get any cash. "You have shit stashed away, Mom...get me some money in my account. Also, see about getting some special foods for me. This stuff here is not what I normally eat. See about having a glass of wine or something added to my meals too.

And not the cheap shit. I want good wines. And some new underthings. All they give me is cotton. I want some silk—"

"Park, did you not just hear me say that I don't have anything? No money, no house, and no credit cards?" He stood up after telling her he was her son, and if she had to, she should make sacrifices. "How? With what?"

He didn't answer her because he was being taken away by one of the police guards. Damn it all to fuck. Where the hell was she going to get money for any of this? Leaving the jail, she stood outside the walls and tried to think. She really didn't have anything. The twenty-five bucks she had left from her stash was it. There wasn't enough for her to buy a good meal, much less expensive wines and put money in his account.

What was a mom to do when her little boy was going without? Joy had no idea, but she'd figure out something. Somehow, she was going to make things better for her son.

~~~

Park was released from his bonds as soon as he was back in his cell. Where they thought he was going to go in the orange suit he was in was beyond him. He hated wearing it where anyone could see him in here, much less in public.

He had no doubts that his mom would make this work for him. She had always made sure that he had the best and that he had all he wanted. It was good, too; he'd have hated to have hurt her over something like money. Sitting on his bed, the only thing he had in his cell besides a commode and a sink, he thought about what he was going to do when he got out of here. First and foremost, he was going to take care of the little cunt that had turned him in, getting him arrested the first time.

The man moving the mop back and forth down the hall

paused in front of his cell. He nearly asked him what the fuck he was looking at when something slid across the floor at him, and then he moved on. Park sat there for several minutes until he heard the door to the area he was in close. Whatever it was, it must have been important for him to get it in here. But Park waited.

Kicking off his shoes, he stood up and stretched. He wasn't going to bend over and pick anything up, knowing that someone would see it. So, just as casually as he could, he curled his toes around the small item and went back to his bed. Not looking at it until later might make him mad with curiosity, but he wasn't going to get caught with it.

Dinner was brought to him about an hour later. He'd asked for a clock, then demanded one, but no one was moving to get it for him. Also, since they'd taken away his cell phone when he'd come in here, he couldn't even look at that to figure out what time of day it was. So, he timed things out by what slop they brought him to eat.

Breakfast was always the same thing. Oats, toast, and a fruit. The fruit changed daily, but was not anything he'd ever put in his mouth. Lunch was a sandwich, usually bologna or ham, a bag of chips, and some vegetables in a bowl that wouldn't have been served in the worst of restaurants as far as he was concerned. Then dinner.

Dinner wasn't anything that much either. So far, he'd had meatloaf, which he detested, turkey and gravy over mashed potatoes, and dressing. He'd also had something called an open faced roast beef thing. Again, meat over mashed potatoes, as well as slices of the ever-present white bread. Drinks ranged from juice to water. No soda, since he told him that he didn't like it.

These people were rude when it came to personal items

85

as well. Even his own brush and other toiletry items had been taken, and he'd been told to make due. Make due? Like that was even possible with the shit they'd handed him. A tube of toothpaste that was only about two inches long, and a brush that looked like they'd picked it up at the dollar store somewhere or they'd bought them in bulk.

It was hours before he could take any kind of moment on the thing that had been slipped to him. Then once he picked it up, he laughed a little when he realized it was a tiny little tube, but inside of that was a printed note. He read it six times before he put it away and lay down on his bed.

"Be ready on the twentieth. Breakout." That was all it said, and he was excited. Breakout, and only four days away. Nearly giddy with relief, he wanted to get up and dance around his cell. His mom, she was slick, she was. Getting him what he needed to be a free man again. As he lay there, trying his best not to look any different, he thought of getting out of there and what he needed to do to make that happen. Since he'd not been asked to contribute to the breakout, he was going to follow someone else's lead. Until, that was, he got out, then it was every man for himself.

It wasn't like there was anything in here that he'd miss or his mom couldn't help him replace. The fact that she'd played it so well, not letting on like anything was going on, had impressed him. He'd not tell her that, of course. He didn't want her thinking she was smarter than him. And while Park knew he wasn't brilliant, he did have some smarts. Like staying out of trouble when it suited him. Like with the women he'd taken to his bed.

There wasn't any reason whatsoever that he should have been put in jail. It was just sex. That was it. And just because he'd not asked first before taking what he wanted, that made him the bad guy. Well, fuck that shit. He was going to make it his mission to take as much pussy as he wanted. Starting with the cunt that had turned him in.

There were other things that he'd done and had gotten off scot-free. Like killing his father. That had been easy to not just walk away from, but to do as well. His mom had never thanked him for it, but since she'd gotten him the poison in the first place, he figured she was okay with it. People, he knew, were a little afraid of him, and Park thought that was just fine by him.

He'd been a pretty good thief too. Breaking and entering homes had been how he'd enjoyed himself with some extra cash. And the street drugs. That had been the most profitable, but also the most dangerous. Park liked danger, but not at the expense of getting a bullet put in his head.

Park had had it made when his mom had married Landon, and the guy was pretty nice too. Or basically a sap. He wasn't sure which most of the time. But the fact that he'd grown a set and had stood up for himself made him hate him and respect him at the same time. The fucker was going to have to go if he thought he was ruling anything at the house. Mom did most of the time, and when she couldn't or wasn't able to, Park could and did step into the role very nicely.

There were things he could sell if he could get his hands on them. The house had been a gold mine of things that were just laying around. Like some of the picture frames, he knew, were worth thousands. There was a silver tea and coffee set, too, he knew he could get something for. He'd not had to resort to taking things while he'd been staying there because money had been easy to get, and plentiful. Now…well, now the tables had turned, and it was well past time that he took what he wanted.

Park couldn't thank his mom. At least not until he was out. Then it would be just the two of them again. After he took a few things from the house, they'd be on the road again. And he'd have to keep his eye out for another moneybags.

While resting on his cheap mattress and his equally cheap blanket, he thought of the things he could take from the house, and who he would contact to fence them. There were several people that he used…most of them weren't friends as much as they were business partners. Friends fucked you over… partners didn't, in his experience.

When his breakfast tray was given to him, he looked it over for things he could pocket. There was always a baggie of cookies, a bottle of water too. Things he might need if he had to hide out for a little while. Eating the nasty shit that they considered food, Park knew that being hungry could get you caught. So, filling his belly with crap was better than nothing.

Lunch came and went, so he did the same thing. Another bottle of water was set under his mattress, the bags of cookies and crackers as well. He thought about wrapping up half his sandwich, but decided that it would never make it for the next three days. It was nasty now; he had no idea what it would be like if it sat around for even a few more hours.

Before dinner time, he wasn't feeling well. He blamed it on the food, then the air around him. As he got sicker, he used his toilet to puke up everything on his belly and collapsed on the floor. Whatever it was, it was making him sicker by the moment. And closing his eyes made his head spin.

Park stayed on the floor until someone came to bring him his dinner. The guard asked him if he was all right, and he leaned over and puked up bile in the commode again. A short while later he was in the infirmary and hooked up to an IV. Christ, he thought, they were going to kill him before this shit, and now he wished for his death to end the misery of being sick. The last thing he remembered was seeing the guy that had mopped his floor, then nothing.

Chapter 7

Lucy moved back and forth in the big rocker. She didn't care for it overly much—the rocking, not the rocker itself—but it was a way to burn off some of the energy she had racing over her body. She needed to get out more, she decided, and quietly turned the page on the book she was reading.

"You do know that I can hear those pages turning like they're set on about fifty on a speaker, don't you?" She smiled and told Allie that she could turn it down. "Yes, I'm sure. But where the hell is the speaker so I can?"

Allie sat up and looked around the room. It looked like a bomb had gone off. Christian had been trying his best to be quiet when he changed, and had left the things he'd worn lying about. Lucy explained that to the younger woman.

"You've been resting for the better part of two days. Nothing like we thought you might, but Denny thinks it's because you're in such good shape that you took it better than most." Allie nodded, then shook her head. "Too much or not enough?"

"I'm not sure. I sort of feel woozy. You know, like I've been given a huge dose of something strong and it's still running through my system." Lucy said that was understandable, but she'd not been given anything. "Where is Christian that he had to dress up? Court?"

"Yes. He hated to leave you, but he'd made a promise to this person that he'd be there for them. Oh, and your parents called last night. I told them that you were getting things ready for them, and they seemed all right with that. Your mother, she's excited to be living without timers. I don't think I understand that."

"My dad. He has this thing about timing stuff. And since they're traveling in an old camper with a smaller water and holding tank, they have to conserve as much as they can. So, he came up with a timing schedule to make sure they didn't run out of room or water." Lucy nodded and smiled. "I'm starving to death. What can I eat now that I'm assuming I'm a cougar?"

"You are, and anything you wish. I would suggest that you start slowly though. Perhaps only half a cow for now, and maybe later you can have two." Allie laughed. "There, you feel better already, don't you?"

"I feel wonderful. Aside from being hungry. And I think I need a shower." Lucy stood up and told her to have at it and she'd see to food. "Lucy, is everything all right? I mean, it kinda threw me to have you here watching me."

"Yes, everything is wonderful considering that there is an idiot out there trying to find my son." Lucy smiled again. "But we're not worried about that too much. We are, after all, cats that can bounce back from most anything."

Lucy helped her stand up. She was getting stronger by the time they got the water turned on and clothing brought in with her. Lucy wanted to stay and help, but Allie said that she had it. Leaving her to it, she reached out to Christian and let him know that Allie was up and about.

Wow, that was quick. Is she all right? Lucy told him she appeared to be. *I have this trial going on today, and I'm thinking tomorrow as well. And I've asked Dad to look into some things with her father's case. Did you know that he lost both his legs in an accident that wasn't even close to being his fault?*

What happened? He told her what he knew so far while she made her way to the kitchen. *I don't understand. He was told to jump on the lift gate to make it go down, and they didn't compensate him for his injuries when it caught and hurt him? That's just not right, son. I hope you can take them to the cleaners.*

Yes, I hope so as well. And they didn't call the police in either. Just called an ambulance, then later the police met him at the hospital. The report says they were negligent, but nothing ever came of it. Lucy asked him if Allie knew what he was doing. *No. I didn't want her to get her hopes up if nothing come of it. But she'll know eventually. Her family will need to tell their side of it. It ruined them, Mom. They lost everything trying to get lawyers to help them, as well as him not able to work and pay the bills. I think that's why they travel, to keep ahead of it all.*

That's so sad. Allie said that the camper that they're in is old and sort of out of shape. Christian told her what he knew about it. *My goodness. A sixty-year-old camper that they have to crank up to sleep in? I'm a cougar with some added strength, but I don't think I could do that nightly.*

Me either, and I love to be out of doors. I've looked into some housing for them close to us. After this, they could afford a better means of transportation, I'm hoping, and a good house, but I'm getting them this one so that they can be near Perry and Allie. She told him how proud she was of him. *They need help and I have the means to do it. And I'm not doing this for them, so much as I am for Allie. I think she would like to have them around more.*

I believe you're right.

Lucy talked to the cook that had been hired for their home and made sure that they knew who to call for repairs if any were needed, as well as how to order foodstuff for the house. Normally she might not have done something like this for one of her sons' homes, but Christian had asked her to do it so that Allie could rest. Who would have thought that she'd be up and around so quickly?

By the time Allie came downstairs, she'd set things up enough that she could take over now. After giving her all the information that had been shared with the new staff, she sat down while Allie ate her lunch. It was bigger than she might have had first thing after waking, but after a quick talk with Denny, she didn't say anything. Apparently, it was fine for her to have whatever she wanted.

"My parents, did Christian tell you about them?" Lucy told Allie that she knew they were having a rough time. "Yes, they are. I'm hoping I can convince them to stick around for a little while. I don't know how much they'll have in the way of things to put in a home, but Christian and I are going to help them."

Lucy didn't tell her about the house…that was going to be up to her son. But she did tell her that there was all sorts of furniture in the barn that was on the back of their property. It was from updates they'd done on their own home a few years back.

"Thank you for that." Lucy said it was her pleasure. "I'm supposed to meet with Dane in a couple of hours. I had no idea that everyone would know I was awake already."

"That would be my fault. I told Denny." They both laughed. "He is such a wonderful man, but there are times when I want to bash his head in. If you ever have a secret, don't tell him. If you do, you might as well have it printed in the paper. The man cannot hold onto anything but with his patients."

"My dad is like that too. Mom used to have to buy our gifts without him or we'd know. Not that there weren't all sorts of hints around about them, but it was his duty to stay out of the wrapping area." Lucy told her that she couldn't wait to meet them. "My mom is very strong. I mean in that she can help a person in ways that you'd never know. And all behind the scenes. Once, when I was away at college, there was a friend of mine who could barely afford her bills each month. Not that we had all that much either, but Mom would bake her an extra pie or take over some soup when there was plenty. We never went without to help, but Mom made sure that if we had it, she did as well."

"They sound like very special people who have very special children." Allie flushed brightly, and Lucy patted her on the hand as she stood up. "I must be off. I have two meetings to go to on the library fundraiser, as well as a couple of other things that need my attention. You do know how to reach Christian, don't you?"

"Yes. Through our link. He startled me in the shower earlier. Thank you for helping me today." She told Allie it was a delight to spend time with her. "And I'm so glad that you're Christian's mom. You've raised good sons that are worthy of you."

"Why thank you, sweetheart. That's the nicest thing anyone has ever said to me."

Kissing Allie on the cheek, Lucy left before she became all teary. She hoped that the rest of the women coming to her sons were very much like the two she had already fallen in love with.

~~~

"Three hundred people are in those African tunnels, and there are more expected to arrive any day now." Allie looked at the aerial map as Dane pointed out what was going on. "I know you've done this sort of work before, helping with the wounded, but if you don't want to help now, I completely understand."

"Don't be crazy. Of course I'll help you." She looked at the map again and thought of the ways in and out of the tunnel. "Tell me again why we want to bring them out of there when they're not hurting anyone or even harming the area."

"The mountain above them is being excavated for limestone. Not as much as there was when they started showing up, but now it's become a large operation. The problems that are occurring now are because of the dynamite that is being used instead of just the drilling. Not that it's not going on now, but it's become more frequent and more dangerous. We've tried to get the company that is doing the mining to halt for a month or so, just until we get the people out, but they said they have deadlines." Brayden continued as he pointed out the markers that were being worked in. "Most of the topmost part of the mountain has been worked over, and that is harming the lower area daily."

"Deadlines. Like that is more important than people. Why are they living in the mountain instead of in the town? I mean, are they literally living in the mountain?" Dane brought out another map and laid it over the first one. She showed her why the people had had to flee. "They flooded the town? What sort of fuckers are these?"

"The worse kind. Hello, little sister." Perry joined the discussion after giving her a tight hug and a kiss on the cheek.

96

He'd come with Julian. "That's where I've been for the last week, just talking. I say that because that's what it feels like, I'm talking to walls and no one is listening. If you don't mind, I have a better plan. But it's not going to make us any friends."

"I'm game." Allie nodded when Dane spoke, just to let him know that she was in as well. "If this involves kicking some ass, I'm even more for it."

"It will involve money. Which, as we've discovered, goes further than kindness." She knew that as well, and looked at the first map when Perry pulled it to the top. "This area is full of animals that aren't near the end of their time, but if this continues then it might as well be. Boar and a few other indigenous animals will run out of land, as well as food, if the destruction of their land is continued. I'd like to propose we try and get someone to buy the land that they're using rather than let them lease it from the current owners."

"How are they doing this without owning the property?" Perry explained that the owners were living in another country and didn't care so long as the rent was on time. "How many acres are we talking?"

"They're using ten thousand, but there is another ten that is set to be used if they need it. And you'll not believe how cheap the land is going for." He told them what he'd been able to find out. "With a few investors, it can be purchased, then the new owners can make their own set of guidelines or make them move. They have a signed agreement with this company, and I have a copy of it. But since I have no idea of the legal wording, I can't tell if the new owners would have to abide by their terms or not."

Allie wasn't sure what her part in all this would be. Even if they had gone in to get the people out, all she'd ever done in this sort of situation before was to help with handing out food and water when everyone was relocated. But getting people out of a mountain who had absolutely nowhere else to go was beyond what she knew anything about. That didn't mean she'd not help, but she wasn't sure about the planning part.

"I can ask Christian to go over it. I mean, I don't know if he can see it either. I don't even know what sort of an attorney he is." Dane told her without looking up from the paper. "General law sounds vague, doesn't it?"

"Usually, but he is very well versed in all sorts of situations. Corporate law is one. There is also estate planning that I know he does, as well as personal injury and accidents. He wanted to be a country lawyer, so he minored in a lot of areas." Allie felt stupid for not knowing this, but Dane smiled at her. "He and you have had a lot going on, so I would imagine that talking about personal things have gotten waylaid."

"Yes, a lot of stuff has." She looked at the contract when it was handed to her. "He's not coming home tonight because he has to file some things up there in the morning. So, do you think I could send this to him somehow?"

"Ask him how he wants it. The sooner the better." She nodded and went into the other room. She was still figuring out this connection thing, and if she messed up, she didn't want them to see it. Her brother would never let her live it down. Smiling, she thought of how much Dane and Brayden had in common when she reached out.

I have a contract here that we might need your help on. Brayden laughed. *I'm so sorry. I'm just getting the hang of this thing.*

No worries. And you should know that I can look it over for you as well. I've traveled a great many countries and have some knowledge of the laws. But we can bring Christian in on this too. Hang on. It was strange, talking to him when she knew that he was at his home. Then when Christian joined their conversation, she smiled again. *Now, read the contract to us and the two of us can take notes. Word for word, okay?*

Yes, I can do that. But there are places on here that are marked for signatures that haven't been signed. Christian asked her to read those first. *Well, to be honest, there are no signatures on it, from either party.*

Where did you get this copy? She said her brother. *Okay, can you get him? I mean, we might have no worries at all.*

After telling Perry to come help her, Dane joined them, and the conversation. Perry could talk to Christian but none of the rest of them because he was still human and he'd only exchanged blood with him. The others were talking as if they were all in the same room.

You got this copy from the courthouse? Perry told them that he had, just that morning. *So, no one signed off on this, neither the owners nor the company using the land. Yet it's been filed. This is great.*

Why? Brayden was still laughing and saying how funny it was when Christian answered her. *Why is it that they didn't check if it had been finalized before they took it to the courthouse?*

Don't know, but it will work in our favor. I'm suggesting that as a family, we buy this land. All of it. That was a lot of money and she told them that. *Yes, but it's also an investment. Not just for us, but the people living there too.*

It was decided in minutes, and Christian said he'd make the call as soon as court was over. When he touched her mind a few minutes later, he assured her that no one could hear them. He asked her how she was feeling.

Great. I was a little off my feet when I woke up, but I'm okay now. He told her that was to be expected. *Also, I'm not sure that this has anything to do with it, but I feel supersized. Like I could take on the world and win.*

That too is normal, I heard. But you can't, not without me nearby to watch. She laughed with him. *I'm sorry that I wasn't there when you woke, but Peter and his wife had been jerked around enough. Her mom left them everything when she passed away, and the second husband wants his share, as in everything. It's been hard on them.*

I bet. And I'm glad that you're helping them. My parents could have used someone like you in their corner all those years ago. He said that he was. *Was what? In their corner? It's too late for helping them, I think.*

It's not. I'm working on it now. I was going to tell you when I got home, but you should know that there is liability against the company on two other claims. I'm going to represent them all and get money for all of them. She asked him why they were being sued by others. *One is the same claim as your dad's, but this man died. And the other is a woman who went into labor at work and they wouldn't let her leave. As in, they stood behind her until she fell to the floor and gave birth there. Her baby sustained injuries and had to be hospitalized for them. He's going to be all right now, but it was scary for them.*

A note was slipped in front of her as she sat at the table. *My parents are pulling in the drive right now. I'll talk to you later, okay?*

Yes, that's wonderful. You go and visit with them, and if they feel like it, when I get back tomorrow, we'll go out to dinner. You think they'll like that? She said that she did. *Good. I'll make the arrangements for that as well. And have fun.*

Going out into the yard to watch them getting out of the camper, she wondered how on earth they'd been able to stay in it. She never realized how tiny the thing was, nor how old. The front part was hanging on by tape, and the windows were cardboard along the left side. As her mom got out of the driver's side and ran to her, Allie did to her as well. Brayden and Perry helped get Dad out and into his wheelchair.

Hugging her mom, she felt the weight of the world seem to be blown away. They talked as they always had, over each other, finishing each other's sentences. And when she went to her dad, he was the same way, sniffling while he spoke, telling her how much he'd missed her. As they were taken in the house, the camper was unloaded by Brayden and Perry, as luggage was all they'd need for now.

"You don't have to do that, dear. We can sleep out there." Her dad huffed at her mom. "Well, we don't want to put them out, Heath. They have enough going on."

"Yes, and us sleeping in the camper isn't going to make a hill of beans after the fact. You tell us where you want us to bunk, darling, and that's where we'll stay." She kissed him on the cheek. "Well, that made us having to drive all night sure worth it."

"You guys are going to have the bedroom on this floor, so Dad doesn't have to mess with the stairs. And it has its own living area for now. There are some renovations going on out at the pool house, but those guys aren't going to bother you." She showed them to their room and let them unpack. "I'm so glad you guys are here. Just come out when you're ready."

Sitting in the big living room with Christian's parents, she realized how things might look to them. Allie told them that her parents were all she had in this world, and didn't want them to think less of them just because they were poor.

"Oh honey, we don't care a fig what their income is, nor where they might lay their hats. They raised you and Perry to be good people and wonderful adults. To me that makes them the richest people we know." She thanked Dr. Stanton. "Please, if you call me Dr. Stanton again, I might have to start calling you Mrs. Stanton."

"All right. Then Denny it is. Also, you should know that my parents are the same way. They'll call you doctor and missus because they'll feel it's their duty, simply because they'll feel less than you." Lucy said that wasn't going to happen. "Just wait. Our parents are pretty stubborn."

"We'll see. I've been known to tangle with the worst of them." They were all laughing when her mom and dad came in the room. "There you are. My name is Lucy, this is my husband, Denny. These are two of our sons, Brayden and his mate, Dane, and Julian."

"My goodness, you're all so large." Her mom flushed when everyone laughed. "I didn't mean that to be insulting."

"No one took it that way, Mom." Perry sat down on the couch next to Allie and their mom as he continued. "The Stantons are family and they are large. But you'll not find better people. They've helped me out of a few jams, and they've hired Allie and me to train some of them in fighting."

"I know that you're all cats...cougars, we were told. So, if you're all that, why do you need special training? You have the best here in my children, but can't you just go ahead and kill whoever is making a show of themselves?" Her dad looked at her. "What I mean is, I'm assuming that you can do whatever you want."

Brayden said that they could. "But, we'd like to see if we can work things out first, even if it's with fists rather than shifting, because that can get all kinds of things involved. The police being one of them. Working with your son and daughter, it's giving us options that we might not have had when out in the public."

"I can see that." Her dad looked at her as he continued. "You've been changed, then? I hope so. From what I've heard, you can heal much quicker and you can be safer. That's what I'm concerned about."

"Yes, I've been converted." Dad nodded. "I only just woke up today, as a matter of fact, and I do feel better. You're okay with it?"

"Of course we are. There isn't any reason for anyone to be upset about you becoming all that you can." He looked at her mom as he continued. "We want nothing more than for you and Perry to be safe. And if this helps that along, then we're all for it."

They talked a bit more, mostly about their trip and how they had managed to stay in some nice places despite the weather. Her dad was worried, she could tell. About what, she didn't know, but she would find out, and soon. She wanted them to be happy here, not worried about anything any longer.

Chapter 8

Joy was waiting in the front lobby of the prison when a man dressed in a suit came out to talk to her. She'd been here for a few hours now, and was ready to have some heads roll. He asked her to have a seat and she did, but she wasn't going to just sit idly by while they kept her from her boy. They were going to know her wrath.

"There's been some trouble." She braced herself for anything then. There was always somebody someplace that would take exception to her son for some reason and hurt him. Everyone just needed to back off and mind their own business. "I'm afraid that as of twenty minutes ago, your son showed up as missing."

"Missing? How did you lose a grown man?" She wasn't sure what was going on, but she hadn't done anything to get him out and she knew that Landon hadn't either. "What do you mean, he's missing? Has he been released and no one told me? I swear to you, if I traveled all the way here and you've released him, I'm going to sue your ass."

"No, it's not that. He and three other men have escaped.

We are narrowing it down, and we believe it happened sometime late last night or earlier this morning."

She tried to think what that would mean for her as the man droned on about how they'd done bed checks and such and he hadn't seemed to be missing then. Something about him being ill and so on. Standing up, he did as well and stopped talking.

"I need to go home." He told her that wasn't going to be possible. "I don't understand you. I drove here and now I'm going home. There isn't anyone else I want to see here, so there isn't any reason for me to hang around any longer. I think you've kept me here quite long enough for no reason."

"I'm afraid that you're going to have to be held for questioning." She asked him about what. "He left a note. For us to give to you. It thanked you for getting him out."

"You read a personal note to me? How dare you." She slapped him across the face and started for the door, but the two guards that had been there when she entered moved to cut off her escape. "You had better make them move, or so help me, I'm going to have their pensions too. This is ridiculous. My son is out there and he might need me. Why are you doing this to me?"

"Have a seat, Joy, and I'll continue." She sat, but she wasn't happy about it. "Your son named you as part of his escape plans. There is not only him thanking you, but also, he wants you to wire him the money that you get when you have your husband killed. That is not going to sit well with a great many people." She asked him what he was talking about. "Park said in the note that you were paying someone to have Mr. Hartman killed, and that the insurance money was to cover the hit. He knew a great many details for us not to be concerned. He left the note in his hospital bed that we

106

had put him in."

"You can be concerned all you want, but I'm leaving here." The man only grinned at her as two more guards joined the first. "I'm not going to be treated this way. I demand that you let me go, and I'll only take your money and not have you fired."

He pulled out some paperwork, along with a small device that could have only been something to record her and him on. When he asked her if he could record her, she just crossed her arms over her breasts and stared. Joy knew that her stare alone could make a man do what she wanted. But apparently not this man, as he simply told her that she had signed a waiver when she arrived that stated that she might be recorded, and he didn't need her verbal permission. This was not going well for her, and she was beginning to get a little nervous.

"There are some questions that we have for you, Ms. Hartman. One of which is your relationship with a man by the name of Jamison Cartwright." She tried to think who that was. "You contacted him some months ago to do a job for you, to kill your husband for the insurance money."

"He's dead." She knew her mistake as soon as the words left her mouth. "What I mean is, I've heard that he's dead. You know how that is, a bad guy gets his comeuppance."

"Mr. Cartwright left a note as well. It seems to me that men around you want to get you into trouble, don't you think?" He let those words hang there for several minutes before he just shook his head at her. "He told, in great detail, how you had hired him to do a job and that he feared for his life. The note went on to say that you hired him to kill your now ex-husband. And that he was afraid that you were going to have him killed by your son."

"What my son does is his own business, and I don't have an ex-husband. I was married long ago, but he died. Landon is all I have now, and he is not my ex anything." This was much worse than her son getting out of jail, and sounding more and more like she was in deeper shit than he'd been. "Why are you questioning me like this? Don't I need a lawyer? Not that I've done anything wrong, but this feels like I'm being accused of something."

"Do you? And I'm not asking you anything you have to answer. You could just sit there if you'd like." She didn't think that was right, but nodded. "Do you want to answer any more questions?"

"No. I mean, I'm not sure what you think I can answer. I came here to see my son. He's not here, and now you're telling me that some man I sort of knew left a note telling you that I had him kill my husband. As far as I know, my husband is on vacation someplace." He reminded her that he was her ex-husband. "He'll change his mind on that soon enough. We had a little fight and he's gone to reflect. I want you to let me out of here. I've done nothing at all wrong."

"Landon Hartman filed all the necessary paperwork to get a divorce from you. And since you didn't show for court, then it's been finalized." She asked him what court date. "The one that was given to you when you were served. And since Mr. Williams recorded the conversation that he had with you at the shop that refused your card, we know that he told you. Amazingly, he was also able to get you beating the snot out of him."

Joy stood up, then sat back down. She didn't remember anyone saying a word about a date, but then she'd been so angry that it might have slipped by her. Trying to think what the fuck she was going to do now, she pulled out her cell phone and made her way through her numbers to find her lawyer. Or at least the only one she knew. But the phone wasn't working.

"I have no service. I need to call my attorney and let him know that you're falsely accusing me of things." The man—she wondered if he'd given her his name or not—said that he had service. "Then I don't know what's wrong with mine. I need to call my attorney. Mr. Stanton."

"Mr. Christian Stanton? He's here. But I don't think he's going to help you either." She asked him why not. "Because he works for Landon, not you. If you'd like to call another attorney, then I can make sure you get—"

"We're still married." He shook his head. "We are. I don't know anything about court dates, and until I hear it from Landon himself, then I'm not going to believe a word you say to me."

"All right." She looked at her phone and could see that it wasn't just out of service because she was in the prison surrounded by thick walls, but it was asking her to call the office to make arrangements, of which she had no money to cover. "Your ex-husband is here. We were awaiting his arrival before we spoke to you. He said that you'd want him, but he's only here to verify that you're divorced. Would you like to speak to him?"

Here? Landon was here? Maybe he was the one that paid to have her little boy released. Or better yet, he was going to tell her that he'd had a change of heart and that he was taking it all back, including her inability to have any place to stay or money to spend. Standing up when the door opened, she stared at her husband and wondered what he'd been up to. He looked like he was glowing with good health.

He was tanned and smiling. His hair was a little longer

than it normally would have been, and he had lost some weight. Not that he'd ever been fat, but she figured that he was on some kind of workout program, something that she'd asked him to do, and had toned himself up. She wondered briefly who he was getting in shape for. Certainly not her.

"Landon, I've missed you so much. Where have you been all this time?" He didn't speak to her, but sat down on the couch next to Stanton. "Are you not speaking to me? After all this time? What have you done with yourself? You've been in one of those dry out clinics, haven't you?"

She wanted to paint a picture of him that made him look bad, but she didn't think it worked when he just grinned and started speaking in a tone she'd never heard from him before.

"Oh yes, I'll talk with you, but I'm not going to tell you anything personal. That's done as far as we're concerned. And I've no reason to dry out, as you put it. I'm not now, nor have I ever been, a drunk. You'd know that too if you cared." She asked him what he meant. "We're divorced. You no longer have any rights to my personal life. Not that you didn't try very hard to make me a dead man, but I'll decide what you need to know or not."

"You're being very rude. These men are asking me things that I don't know anything about." He just sat there and she wanted to scream at him. So instead of doing that, she turned to Stanton. "You're a very hard man to get in touch with as well. Have you told your secretary to screen your calls concerning me?"

She'd meant it as a joke, but he said that he had. "It was very easy, as a matter of fact. She doesn't like you any more than I do. And you and I have no business relationship as of the moment that Landon filed for his divorce. I'm here on his behalf, not yours."

"You can't do this to me. They're accusing me of things that I didn't have anything to do with. I need an attorney." Stanton told her that was something she'd have to work out with the judge. "I'm not going to trial. Someone has to help me. I'm not going to jail or trial over these lies."

"Oh, but you will be." She stared at Christian, using her best, "I'm pissed" stare, and he laughed at her. "You can try that all you want, but it doesn't change the facts, Joy. You're going to jail, where you will await trial, and then hopefully, if I'm as good as I hope, go to prison. For a very long time."

This wasn't going well. She was being held for no reason that they should know about. Her son, her little boy, was out there somewhere and he would need her. The fact that they were telling her that he'd left a note, accusing her of all sorts of things, wasn't right either. Park would never do that to his mom. She asked to see the note, and was given a copy of it with the word evidence stamped on it.

"How do I know that you didn't write this to try and trip me up?" She knew it was her son's handwriting. Park never could spell well, and he would always write escape *excape*. "I don't know why you think this has anything to do with me. I just got here. If I had helped him to get out, then why would I come to visit my little boy? Landon, you have to fix this for me. I'm your wife."

"No, you are not. You're not in my will either. The insurance has been changed as well. So even if you were to kill me, which I highly doubt that you could afford now, you'd get nothing." Joy asked him why he'd do such a thing to her. "Because you're no longer my wife. And I have made sure that the world knows it. As of today, it's front line newsworthy. That, and you've been arrested for attempted murder, conspiracy, as well as a whole lot of other things."

"You can't do that to me, Landon. I'm your wife." He stood up and she did as well. But instead of getting to follow him out the door, she was put in cuffs and read her rights. "Landon, get back here. We have to talk about this. I can't afford to be without funds. You owe me. I'm your wife."

"You keep saying that, and I keep telling you that you are not any longer, thankfully." Landon was laughing as the door closed behind him. What on earth could he find that was so funny? She was stuck there, and he wasn't helping.

~~~

Park wasn't happy. Not that he had expected his escape to be without consequences, but this was bordering on insane. He looked at the chain that was still attached to his ankle and wondered what the hell he was supposed to do now. There would be no help from the morons that he got out with, either. They had left him high and dry.

He wasn't clear on the way they'd gotten out. He'd been sick, thinking that he'd been poisoned and was about to die, when he was picked up and taken somewhere dark. Park had tried to speak, but his mouth had been taped and his hands tied. And no amount of struggling had gotten him free. Then when he'd woken up this morning, he was alone and the note left for him simply said "You're on your own now." They'd also left a cell phone that was so cheap, it wouldn't even take pictures. And a pile of clean, inexpensive clothing. What the fuck did that mean, he was on his own?

Trying to call his mom had netted him nothing. Her phone was out of service. He had no idea what that was supposed to mean either. Did she not know that he'd want to find her? And he had left her a note, or thought he had. There had been a pen in his hand and someone telling him what to say, but as far as actually writing it, he had no memory of doing so. It was all a bit fuzzy.

"Where the fuck are you?" He wasn't sure who he was talking to or about. He needed answers, and wasn't happy that he wasn't getting any. Nor did he have any idea how he was supposed to get them.

As he looked out the window of the dirty house he was in, he saw Stanton and another man. It took him several seconds to realize it was his dear old stepdaddy. That man had been a pain in his ass since he'd gotten out of prison. He had cut him off, taken away his cars and credit cards, and told him he was on his own. He'd not liked it any better at the time than he did now. He'd not been on his own once since he'd been born. There had always been someone around to pick him up, dust him off, and give him some cash. Even going to his mom had done nothing for his situation. Not even she could get him cash.

As he watched the two men, he was amazed at how good Landon looked. Like he'd been on a holiday and gotten laid several times. Park wondered if his mom was buttering him up, and that was how he'd been sprung. But that didn't sound right either. Landon had been really pissed off, and not just at him.

Park had heard them fighting before all this went down. Mostly his mom yelling that she wasn't going to be treated like this. His mom had a good head on her shoulders and knew how to make a man do what she wanted, but all her tricks didn't seem to be working in her favor now. Perhaps she was just too old. He'd noticed that recently as well, how much his mom was beginning to look her age.

Park had told her that once. He'd never do that again either. She had been so mad at him that she'd not spoken to him for an entire week. Park hadn't realized how much he needed his mom until then. But he wasn't going to let her walk all over him either.

Keeping an eye out for Landon, he noticed that a great many people seemed to know him. He hardly made it more than a few feet before he was turning around and talking to someone else. Even coming out of the storefronts that he went in and out of with ease, he would wave at someone driving by and chat a bit.

It was one of the things that he hated most about the man... his ability to adapt to situations and to befriend anyone. He'd even tried to be Park's best bud at first. It seemed, however, that the more he pushed the man away, the harder he would come back, smiling and acting like nothing had come between them. Then he'd gotten caught.

"You'll not live here anymore after you return home. If you were to return." He said that he'd not done anything to those women. "Yeah, and I can fart unicorn dust from my ass. You're as guilty as they come and we both know it. But I won't have you here. Not after this. You're not welcome."

"Yeah? Well, we'll see what my mom has to say about that, now won't we?" Landon only sat there, his face set. "You really don't want to fuck with me, Landon. I know a lot of people that can make your life a living hell."

"It already is." He stood then and Park backed from him. Landon was a formidable man, and had on several occasions frightened him. "You see if I'm not serious. Come around and you do so at your own risk."

He had left him there, sitting in the unflattering orange and green jumpsuit. His mom had returned, every day, to the point that he was sick of seeing her. And she never had any good news. Even after he was transferred, she kept coming, driving the two hours each way to see him. Park didn't realize how much he would have missed that part now until now, when she was no longer seeing him all the time.

Park needed a better cell phone. He thought it was the cheapness of it that was keeping him from making the necessary calls, but wasn't sure. But to get one would mean going into a store. And having something to purchase it with. He was thinking that he could more than likely get in and out with one, but being seen might cause some uproar. That made him think of how he got out of the stupid prison in the first place.

He'd been sick. So sick that they'd hooked him up to an IV, as well as put a plastic sheet under him. Nothing was staying down or in him. After shitting himself twice, he remembered someone giving him a shot. Of what, he didn't have a clue, but he did fade out. And when he woke, he was here. And Park had no idea where here was. Looking harder out the window, he saw a street sign and nearly laughed. He was perhaps five blocks from Landon's house. Going to the ground level, he glanced around before crossing the street and hiding in the alley. Carefully, he made his way to the next street, then the next.

Park decided he was getting into Landon's house—he knew where the hidey key was—then he'd steal what he needed, and get out of town. After he found his mom. Then they'd be free to start their little endeavor over again. Finding a rich man to support them both in a way that felt good.

However, at the rate he was going, it would take him a long time to get home. An hour later, he was only a block and a half away from the building he'd been in. Sneaking around buildings, he'd gotten lost twice and had to backtrack to get to where he knew the street. But he had made a horrific discovery.

Signs were posted everywhere with his name and picture on them, asking people to be on the outlook for him. Rewards were offered with phone numbers to call if they saw him. Park stared a little too long at his face in the picture and was nearly caught there. Putting his head down, he took off.

"Armed and dangerous. Where the fuck did they think I was going to get a gun? They don't hand them out to people when they escape. Morons. I swear, people get dumber every day." He looked up when someone laughed and saw Landon. He was only a few feet away.

"Yes, I heard that as well. Joy will be in jail for some time, I'm thinking." Park paused, and then moved closer to the shadows beside the building that Landon was in front of. He couldn't hear the other person speaking, but Landon was as clear as day. "Murder. Attempted murder. There are some charges of fraud, as well as conspiracy. Her court date is set for three months from now."

Three months? That explained a lot. She wasn't calling him or meeting him simply because she was in jail. He wanted to go and ask Landon about it, but the man wasn't going to be helpful. Not at this late date. So, Park listened.

"No, no. That's all been taken care of. Christian filed the necessary paperwork just the other day. We're divorced, and she and her boy have been taken out of not just my will, but there is no insurance for her to collect on either." Park felt the slow burn of his temper slide over him. Landon continued talking. "Yes, I did get some rest in. Spent a lovely two weeks in France, and then traveled a bit more. I'm only here to make sure that she knows that we're done. And that ad in the paper, that helped as well. I changed benefactors as quickly as I did all the locks on my home and property. Gotta see a guard at the end of the driveway to even get on the land I own."

116

Park tried to see who he was talking to, but all he could see was darkness in the car. If there was anyone in there he thought, they were short. He was trying to move his body around to see if he could get close enough to Landon to swipe his wallet when another man joined him. After a brief hug, the two of them started walking away.

Mom was in jail. The insurance that she swore would be part his was no longer a viable option for them. No will was naming him as heir, and he didn't have access to the house either. What the fuck was he supposed to do now?

Park made his way back to the building he'd been in. There wasn't any food there, so as he made his way past the grocery store, he pocketed a few of the apples and oranges that were on display there.

Keeping his head down, he detoured into a gas station and into the bathroom. There he found some towels as well as a roll of toilet paper. He didn't know what he was supposed to do with the latter of the two things, but he took them anyway. And as he left, he bumped the snack machine hard enough to knock it over, and took what he could lay his hands on before someone came to see what was going on. Getting back to the building had him breathing hard, but he knew he had a bounty of food now.

"Six bags of chips, three candy bars, as well as some hippy shit." He opened the package of dried pumpkin seeds and tried them, but quickly spit them out. "Who the fuck eats this shit?"

It didn't even come close to filling his belly, but it did take the edge off. Park wanted a steak and baked potato, with a nice wine and a thick slice of cheesecake for dessert. All he had for his efforts was a dry mouth from the chips, and a nut from one of the candy bars stuck in his tooth. Fuck, this is harder than being in jail, he thought to himself.

Chapter 9

"And this tracker, it keeps track of him no matter where he is?" Christian nodded and then shook his head at Dane. "I don't understand that answer. Does it or not?"

"Yes, it does. Unless he goes some place that doesn't have service. This thing works on Wi-Fi. So, without it, we don't get a signal. But so far, he's stayed pretty much where we had him dropped." Landon joined them in the dining room and laughed. "You did really well today. I would have thought you were having an honest conversation with someone."

"Felt like a fool, if you want to know the truth. Talking to an empty car like I was." He thanked Allie for the glass of tea she handed him. "I took care of the theft that he did at the Gas and Go. He didn't get much. The really stupid thing was, there were boxes of candy and stuff sitting right there by the thing that he didn't even bother with. What a fool."

"Well, we already knew that part." Landon nodded and sipped his tea. "He is aware now of the will, as well as the insurance policy. Also, that his mom is in jail. Now we just wait."

"Why are we doing this?" He looked at Allie and she flushed. Taking her hand in his, he asked her what she meant. "Why are we just following him around and not having him arrested? I mean, we know where he is at all times because we put that implant thing in his back when we put him in the infirmary. He's stolen food, we saw him do that. Why are we waiting? Or for that matter, why did we get him out in the first place?"

"If they arrest him now, it's only going to put additional years on his sentence for leaving prison. We all are aware of that. And what's to say that in a few years, less than when he was in the first time, he figures out a way to get out? And starts all over, this time where we can't get to him or find him." She nodded, but still looked confused. "We want him to face penalties that will put him in a deep hole. Not death, but in a prison that will have him locked up and locked down for a very long time. Where he'll only see daylight for an hour a day. Have no contact with anyone other than a single guard. That way, we hope, he'll never get out again to hurt another living person."

He asked her if she understood now. "Yes, I think so. And this prison, you're sure that he'll make it there? I'm not saying that you're not on the right track here, but he has slipped through the cracks on more than one occasion."

"We have a plan. With your help, if you want." Allie tightened her grip on his hand as she looked at Dane when she continued. "I can become whatever I want. Did you know that?"

"Yes, into anything with a heartbeat." Dane shifted. He'd seen her do it before this, but it always made his heart a little jumpy to see it. "Holy fuck. You're him."

Dane had mastered shifting so much so that she could

become anything, including things without a heartbeat. But right now, she stood before them as Landon Hartman. And when Landon moved beside her, there wasn't any way to tell them apart. When Dane shifted back, she sat down beside them. Looking at Allie, she told them what her plan was.

"You and I, if you're willing to help, will go about town. Me as Landon and you as yourself. Landon has already established that he's back and takes walks. You and I will do that enough that Park will make his move. And he will, we think, now that he knows that he's getting nothing and his mom isn't going to be of any help either." Allie asked her why they thought Park would make a move. "He's going to be desperate soon. No money, no food, and he can't have gotten those chains off either. The couple of people who did see him said that he was dragging them behind him. He's not going to like that."

"And you think what? That he'll try and kidnap us? Maybe.... You believe he'll hold him for ransom, and I'll be the one that he can bargain for if no one helps with Landon." Dane shook her head and looked at Christian. He wasn't sure he was going to like this plan any better than Allie was. "Tell me, damn it."

"We think that in his mind, you're the one that caused all this. It's easy to see that his downfall started and ended with you and Landon." Christian nodded when Allie did. "He'll try and ransom you both, or you and I in this, but we're going to give him ample opportunity to write his own ending in his life. And we can get out better than Landon could."

"Because of what we are." Dane nodded. "Okay, but there is something else you should be aware of. I don't know if this is normal or not with converted adults, but I figured out yesterday morning that I can shift too, like Dane."

When she stood up, he let her hand go. It frightened him on so many levels that she was going to do this. Christian didn't have any idea what it might be, but he had a feeling that it was going to be life changing for them both.

When she shifted, her body simply becoming a cougar, he let out a long breath that he'd not realized he'd been holding. Then she shifted again, and continued until he was dizzy with it. Her cougar was beautiful, but the hawk, snake, and then the barn owl had him staring in awe. Dane looked at him.

"I had no idea." He nodded and stood up, but had to sit again. "When you converted her, we all thought that giving her our help would make it so that she could talk to us all. I had no idea that I could pass along my abilities to her."

After converting her and while she was resting, Brayden and Dane had come to him and asked about giving a little of themselves to Allie so that she'd be stronger. And she could, as Dane had said, talk to them all if she needed them. Once Brayden had given her a drop of his blood, Dane had then done the same. It was innocent enough, but apparently much stronger than any of them had ever imagined.

"This isn't normal, is it?" Christian shook his head, then smiled at her. "What? You know something, what is it?"

"You're able to keep your clothing, for one thing." Christian laughed and then stood up. "I want you to hold something in your hand. It doesn't matter what it is, but hold it then shift. I need to know if you can carry anything and have it when you shift."

"Okay." Dane handed her a weapon. "I don't think this is going to be necessary for this, do you?"

"Yes. If you can shift and carry something as heavy and full of metal as this is, it will go a long way in making you safe. And so you know, I have a better plan if you can." Christian didn't ask. If Dane was thinking of a better way, he was all for it if it kept her and Allie safe. "Go ahead, become a hawk again. I love birds. And I want you to see if you can fly as well."

"Okay." Allie looked at him then kissed him on the mouth before becoming a hawk. When she flew around the room, he marveled at how well she'd done it, and then when she landed on the floor again, taking her body, she handed the gun to Dane.

"This is going to be epic." Christian pulled Allie into his arms and held her while Dane paced the room, seemingly talking to herself as no one had time to answer her questions or comments. "No, no, that won't work. But if I can.... Yes, that'll do that, and when.... Yes, I think this will fall into place.... Shit, never thought of that. Well fuck. Okay, this has to be it."

Allie turned to him. "If you don't mind, I'd very much like to have something to eat before I get to the point where I can't enjoy dinner because I'm so tense." Dane laughed and told them it was fine with her. "Good. You'll join us then? All of you?"

"Yes, I'll call in the rest of the family and we can go over this as best we can. But you have to know, I think this plan is foolproof. None of us will be hurt, and even with—"

"No more." Dane laughed as she made her way to Brayden. Christian looked at Allie. "You and I, we're going to have to talk about this. And so you know, if I can do this as well, I'm going to kick someone's ass."

They were all laughing as they gathered around the room. Christian didn't know what was going to go down, but he'd be glad to have it all behind him. There was plenty to do, he knew that, but knowing that there was a plan and safety was foremost, he felt easier about it.

~~~

Allie wandered around the bedroom while waiting on Christian. She didn't know what was going to happen when they spoke, but she knew it was long overdue. There were things he needed to know, and she was sure he wasn't going to like a couple of them. When he entered the room with her, she heard the click of the door lock.

"Your parents are in heaven. The rooms that you had set up for them are perfect, and your dad is having no trouble getting around the house." She nodded and he moved away from the door toward her. "Your mom, she has it in her head that she's going to be cleaning our house for room and board. I set her straight."

"Good luck with that one. I've been trying to tell her that it's fine since they arrived. She thinks they're mooching off us." He nodded and started taking off his tie. "Do you ever wear jeans and a T-shirt?"

"All the time, but I hurried home today so that I could be with you, and didn't take the time to change." She nodded. "Are you all right?"

"Yes, I mean, no. I don't know." He nodded as if he understood. "I had some money saved up and I bought a house. They put your name on the deed as well. I'm sorry about that. But I couldn't afford to do it without your name on it."

"I know. The bank called me while you were there. I had plans of doing just that. I'm assuming that you did it for your mom and dad." She told him she had. "Good. I've also hired them a staff. Not as many as are here...I don't know what your mom wants to do. A cook for the household and a nurse for your dad for sure. And there is no yours and my money,

Allie. It's all ours."

"You have a lot." He said that they had a lot. "I've never been.... What are you doing? You're supposed to be upset with me for going ahead and spending your money."

"Our money. And why would I be upset about you providing for our family?" She sat down, then stood up. "You're as nervous as a mouse in a lab about to be injected with some kind of drug. What's up?"

"My abilities. They're not normal. Does that sicken you?" He frowned at her and stopped moving. "I only just found out about it, and thought that you'd be upset with me because I wasn't like you. I mean, I can become a cat as you can, but all these other things too. I can.... Well, I can make a knife here too." She put out her hand to show him, but he shook his head and told her he believed her.

"I'm in love with you, Allie. I don't care if you can become a one-eyed purple people eater, so long as you come back to me at the end of the day. However, that does have me thinking of weird things you can become." He moved again, gliding across the room while he tossed his shirt away. "I want you."

"Yes, I do you as well." She pulled her sweater off and dropped it on top of his things. "Becoming a cat, it's like having this being inside making me want to do all sorts of things I'd never tried before."

He stopped moving again. "Like what? Tell me what it is your cat is wanting you to do to me. Please?"

Allie laughed. "To you? Okay, to you. Well, for one, she would like for me to make you come down my throat. I think that one might be all me, but who cares, right? Then there is the way she wants me to shift, lick you all over, then have you take me as your cat too. I think that one is all her. She seems to think that you need to mark us both."

"My cock hurts." Laughter spilled from her mouth as she dropped to her knees in front of him. "You're going to be very disappointed if you make me come too quickly. I'm close enough now to just come all over you."

"That would be fantastic." Standing again, she stripped off the rest of her clothing, slapping his hands away when he tried to help. "No, no touching until I have my fun. And then when you're ready, I want you to jerk off and come all over me. I think that alone would make me come hard enough to scream."

Allie unbuttoned his dress pants then lowered the zipper. He was thick and hard, and she could see a stain on his boxers from the leakage at the tip of his cock. Licking the length of him, she heard him hiss through his teeth before curling his hand around the back of her head. Taking him into her mouth, she moaned at the wonderful taste of him.

"Holy Christ, love. That's it." Christian rocked into her mouth, past the tight muscles at the back of her throat. The harder he slid down her throat, the more she enjoyed it as well. "I'm so close. Christ, so very close."

He pulled from her and stood over her. Allie opened her mouth, waiting for him as he fisted his cock above her. And when the first heated cream touched her mouth, she cried out with her own release. The more he gave her, the more she seemed to need.

Christian jerked her up from the floor, but she was weak with need. Her knees were wobbly, her hands even shook. But before she could get steady on her feet, Christian had pressed her head to the bed and was slamming deep inside her pussy from behind. She came twice before he leaned over her, his cock still taking her to incredible heights, and he bit her deep on the shoulder.

126

The darkness swamped her. Then there was bright light, like a star had come into their room and completely bathed it. As her body came back to itself, she felt the room tighten with magic and knew that Christian's cat had taken him.

The bed became her crutch. She was on it, yes, but moving had her feeling like she was made of jelly. Rolling onto the bed, she had barely laid back when the cat was nudging her legs apart and taking her. Allie screamed so hard that she knew that she was going to have a sore throat tomorrow.

No matter how many times she begged him to stop, insisting she had no more in her, he continued to lick her, eat her like she was his last meal and he was going to make it a memory that neither would forget. Finally, when her body was nearly to exhaustion, she pulled the cat up and he snarled at her.

"No more. Please. Unless you're trying to kill me, no more." Falling back on the bed, she closed her eyes. Arms folded her to a warm hard chest. Christian had her. She knew regardless of what happened, he would protect her. Closing her eyes, Allie simply fell over the edge.

When she woke, the room was lighter, like the sun was just coming up. Rolling to her side, she found a beautiful pink rose and a note. Smelling the fragrant flower, she opened the note to read it.

If I could have, I would have stayed in bed all day with you. However, duty calls. There are some phone calls that I would like for you to make for us today. Mostly setting up a time for you to go into the bank to fill out the signature cards. Then later, we can meet for lunch. If you're awake. I love you, Christian.

Stretching, she got up and made her way to the bathroom. She also had to take her parents around to the new house and find furniture for them. Lucy said she had a great deal, and would have the boys take it over when they decided what they'd need. Excited, she dressed hurriedly after her shower and made her way down the stairs.

The house was silent. She wasn't sure what was going on, but there wasn't anyone in the kitchen nor in any part of the house that she went through. Allie was almost afraid to reach out to find anyone, but did call out to Christian. Something was very wrong, she thought.

No one? She told him that she'd gone through the house and there wasn't a soul around. *They were there when I left. Maybe they're in the yard. The gardeners were supposed to come by today and make sure that the gardens would be ready for spring. Go see if you can find any of the people working in the yard.*

She picked up the butcher knife that had been laid on the block, then put it back. She didn't know what was going on, but she certainly didn't want to hurt anyone should there be nothing to worry about. Making her way out to the garage when there didn't seem to be anyone in the yard, Allie felt her cat run over her skin.

The door to the garage was ajar. She tried to look inside, but there was only darkness. Not a sound was coming out, but all sorts of images were running through her mind. A killer with a long knife. There was going to be a clown with scary makeup on. She was ready to run back to the house when she remembered she was a frigging cougar.

"I'm coming in and I'm unarmed." Nothing, not one thing inside or out made a noise. Her skin was crawling with fear as she threw open the door and the lights came on.

Allie screamed. Her body tense with fear and adrenaline, she lashed out with her hand when she felt it morph. Someone screamed back at her, and she felt the room tilt and move. Then she was pulled into arms, strong arms that held her like.... Looking up, she saw that Christian had her, and she sobbed into his chest.

"There are monsters in here." He laughed and she looked up at him again. Slapping him on the chest, she told him it wasn't funny. He lifted her chin and looked into her face.

"Happy birthday, Allie." She must have looked confused because he started to explain. That was when she looked around. The garage was full of family and friends, and everyone was smiling. "Your parents planned this. And I thought...well, I did think it was a good idea myself until you cut me."

"Oh no. I hurt you." She looked at the tears in his shirt and then looked at his skin. There were three long scratches on his chest, just below his nipple. "I'm so sorry. I didn't know."

"Its fine, honey. It really is. I'll just shift and it'll be like nothing happened." Allie nodded and smiled. "Happy birthday, love. Welcome to your party."

The doors were opened up and everyone started to wander around. There was a tent set up behind the house that she hadn't noticed with food and all kinds of drinks. And in the middle of one of the tables was a large birthday cake with plates and other desserts all around it. The line was forming when Christian took her aside.

"You okay with this?" Nodding, she told him she was just fine. "I'm glad. They didn't have any idea who to invite, so we invited everyone. My mom and dad said this was much better than any party she'd ever planned for one of us."

"It's beautiful. And as you know, such a surprise." She took a plate of cheese and crackers when it was handed to her. "I've never had a party before. I mean, maybe when I was a baby there was one, but I don't remember it."

"I hope you're okay with the rest of this as well." She

smiled and told him she was game for anything right now. "Good."

He got down on one knee and pulled out a beautifully wrapped box. She told him to get up, but he took her hand into his. Kissing the back of it, he opened the box and held it out to her.

"Allison Jane LaRue, will you do me the greatest honor and marry me? Today? Before all these people?" She looked around, then back at him. "I'm serious, love. There is a preacher here to do the deed and everything if you say yes."

"Yes. Yes, I'll marry you." Standing, he put the engagement ring on her finger and she nearly fell back from it. "Oh Christian, this is beautiful."

"Not as beautiful as you are. Now, we're going to do this right." Everyone joined them when the man of the cloth came to stand before them. "You aren't going to get a chance to change your mind, so we're doing this right now."

Within minutes, they were man and wife. And when Christian kissed her, she felt like she'd been given the greatest gift of all time. A man to love her, family close, and her first birthday party. Allie was content.

Chapter 10

Christian sat in the courtroom and listened to closing arguments. The other attorney, Daniel Wares, seemed to be recapping every word that he'd said, from the opening comments to the very end. Christian looked over at Beth and Wayne and hoped this went well for them. It was literally everything they wanted.

Six months ago, Beth's sister, Janie Petrel, was in a horrific car accident that killed her and her husband. One of her three children was killed as well, and the other two were injured. Beth and Wayne Buckley stepped in, and made sure that things were taken care of for the family. Then when the kids were released, they took them into their home and cared for them. Adopting them seemed the next step in their lives.

But then a month ago, Janie's ex-husband decided that he should take the children, as well as the insurance money that came with them. The four million dollar policy, the house, the car, and all the contents of the home were what he really wanted. For him, his new wife, as well as their three children.

Wendell had not just a criminal record, but had also

just been released from prison. The children that he had at home now were a mixture of his, hers, and theirs. They were crammed into a two-bedroom apartment that was federally subsidized by the government, and neither of them worked. It wasn't a place that these children would get the kind of loving that they needed and had with their aunt.

"Your Honor?" He glanced to the back of the courtroom when everyone else did. A young courier was there with a messenger bag on his shoulder. Mr. Petrel was on the stand, telling the courtroom some bullshit story about how he was going to make their lives better and that with the money, he and his wife would set up funds for the kids so that they could go to college if they wanted. "Your Honor, I have something that is important to this case."

"You do know that we're in the middle of testimony, don't you?" The young man nodded, but held up the next day air envelope for him to see. "Bring it here then. Court is recessed for one hour."

Christian told the couple to go and get some lunch, that he had to call his wife. And as he was pulling out his phone, Judge Machel came out to ask him and Wares to join him in his office. Christian went, but Wares had to bitch about it.

"When I ask you to come into my chambers, it's not so much a request as you're expected to get up off your lazy ass and get in there. I've had about enough of your shenanigans, and I expect you to get your crap together or you'll be an unemployed attorney." Christian nearly laughed at the expression on Wares' face as Machel continued. "This isn't going to bode well for your client, Mr. Wares. Not well at all."

The judge sat down and waited for them to get settled. Christian hadn't any idea what was going on, but he was slightly nervous waiting on the phone call to end that Machel took while they were seated. Then he felt the touch of Dane.

You should know that I'm helping you out, and wondering what is going to be my bail amount when I'm caught. Then he asked her what she'd done. *Nothing illegal. Sheesh, why would you jump to that immediately?*

Because I know you. Are you responsible for me being in the judge's chambers with an envelope that was just brought to him? She said that she was. *And what, pray tell, is it going to do for me?*

Your Mr. Petrel is a naughty boy. The video you're about to witness, because I'm hoping that's what he is going to do, is show you, is about the man taking what does not belong to him. Plus, and this is the real kicker, there is testimony from one of his kids telling how Daddy dearest raped him on a few occasions. There are reports to back that up too. He asked her what sort of reports. *Medical records. And from doctors as well. The kid had no problem telling on him, and then about a week later, he ran off without any word. I found him. Wasn't hard, but he's been telling me all sorts of things. Most of which is on the recording, as well as evidence to back up the accusations. Robbery. Theft, as well as a few insurance frauds. Like I said, he's been a very bad man.*

Thank you. She said it had been her pleasure, but a lot of the information had been found by his wife. *Allie? How did she know to look?*

Don't know. She came to me this morning and told me that she had an idea and wanted help in looking for it. It's amazing what you can find when you have unlimited resources as well as someone determined to find it. He said the judge was hanging up the phone now. *Yes, and don't be surprised if he tells you that he was called by none other than the Feds. They're there to pick up Petrel and his wife.*

"All right, gentlemen, we have a very serious situation

here. One that is going to end badly for your client, as I said, Mr. Wares." Wares looked shocked, but asked what it was. "Instead of going through the question and answer stuff that I know you're going to have for me, I want you to watch this. And bear in mind, this was dated just two nights ago."

The recording was as clear as day, of a storefront that was obviously closed up for the night. Then a man walks into the front of the camera and looks right at it. It was Petrel. Then his wife did the same. Pulling a large hammer out of a backpack, he looks at the camera again and then smashes in the window.

Both of them run in and then are seen coming out with armloads of merchandise. Most of it is electronics, the rest is unknown as it is in bags. The entire incident takes less than three minutes, and they are both gone before the police arrive two minutes later.

No one spoke as the clerk that worked for the judge handed out files. As soon as Christian opened it, he closed it again and let out a long breath. They were photos of the rape victim that the ER doctor had taken.

"Hard to see, I know. But there are reports, too, to go along with them. Doctor signed statements, as well as other items of interest. There are also reports of the Petrel's claiming fraudulent claims against their neighbors. His neighbor was smart enough to get an outdoor camera on his home to record the goings on at his own place, and caught a few things in the other backyard." Wares started to complain about how this was going to hurt his client's chances of getting the children. "Hurt his chances? Are you looking at the things I just gave you? He's going to jail. Both of them are. And that will leave those other children in the system. I have no choice in this—not that there was much of one anyway—but I'm going to rule in favor of the Buckleys in this. Christ, this is a nightmare, if you ask me. What did your client hope to gain in this? Money?"

"I would imagine that he would have used it for good." Judge Machel just glared. "Your Honor, they surely could use this money for their own defense."

"So, you're wanting me to award them the children, even though I just showed you that they robbed a store and other things. And the money should go to them, so that when they go to prison they'll have money to pay for you to represent them? What about the kids? You do know that if I were to do it your way, there would be five children without parents or money, don't you?"

"They can set up someone to watch over the children while they're taking care of this. I'm sure that we could help them find reasonable care." Machel just stared at him. "You must know someone that could help."

"I do, as a matter of fact." Christian started to object, but was told that it was a done deal. "I'll see the two of you in the courtroom in thirty minutes. And I swear to Christ, if you tell anyone what transpired in here, I will not only have you put in jail, but I'll make sure that you're caged with all sorts of animals like you are."

The courtroom started filling up about ten minutes later. Christian wasn't sure where this was going, but he was a little nervous. If he lost this, and he wasn't sure if he would or not, then there would be a lot of heartache when this was done.

Everyone stood up when the judge entered the courtroom. Christian held Beth's hand and she held her husband's.

"All right then. I've made my decision. Its perhaps one of the easiest ones that I've ever made. I think that every child should be with their parent when possible. I find it to be good for a child to be raised with at least one of them, and in most circumstances, it makes for healthier and happier families."

Christian felt Beth's hand tighten around his. "But in this case, I think that would be a total mistake. And I award full custody to Beth and Wayne Buckley, as well as any and all insurance policies that were to accompany the children of Janie Petrel. The last testament of Janie will stand as well. The children and their caregivers will have it dispersed accordingly."

"That ain't right. You can't take stuff from me when she was my wife." Wares tried to get the other man to have a seat, but he was screaming at the judge about how unfair it was and that he wasn't going to sit still for it. "You just wait and see. I'm going to go over your head on this. I deserve that money on account'a I'm the one that made them babies."

"Yes, you are, and thankfully they didn't have anything to do with you in their formative years." The police came to stand around Petrel. "It is with great pleasure that I tell you that you are under arrest. These men will explain what it is you and your lovely wife are being taken in for. Mr. and Mrs. Buckley, I'd like a word with you two, if you don't mind."

"Yes, sir." Christian hugged them both and asked if they wanted him to go with them. "If you'd not mind. I don't know what he is going to say to us, but I'd like to have somebody there to help us should we need it. I can't thank you enough for this. Those kids…well, we can't have any of our own, and we've grown very fond of these little ones. My sister did a good job for them, and we're going to make sure that they have all they need."

"It was my pleasure. I'm very glad that things went our way." He asked about the arrest. "I'm not at liberty to tell you that. I'm sorry, but I can tell you that you won't have to worry about either of them again."

They followed the judge into his chambers again. There were other people in the room this time, including a woman that looked like she was from children's services. Christian had no idea why he thought that, but when introduced, that was who she worked for. A man was there too, a banker, as well as a notary.

The judge told them that the inheritance from the estate would be coming their way soon. He'd make sure of it. The house would be put in their name as well, and Christian said he'd take care of that as soon as the ruling was finished. After that, the judge sat back in his chair.

"The children of your brother-in-law are going into the system. Today." Beth started crying softly and Wayne held her. "I can't go into great detail about it, but suffice it to say, they'll be separated and put into other homes, if adopted at all."

"We'll take them." Wayne glanced at his wife, and when she nodded he looked at the judge again. "It'll be a hardship, but nothing we can't handle. They'll be loved like they're our own, and not want for affection or compassion."

"I figured you'd say that. And I'm glad for it. While I was finishing up the paperwork in here during lunch, I made a few calls. There will be money from the state for you for caring for them. It's been cleared so that it comes to you immediately as well." Wayne said that wasn't necessary. "But it is. And the state will be mighty glad for you to take them off their hands simply because they'll stay together as a family. Starting right away you'll have what you need to care for them. Any medical you need—including mental health issues they might have—will be yours. Also, there is a friend or two of mine that will help you with an expansion on the home you are getting. There are four bedrooms now, but you'll need a bit more room to grow in. Having a houseful, that's going to take some getting used to, I think."

"Yes, sir, it will, but I'm thinking that it won't be anything compared to what they might have gone through should we have left them in the system." The judge agreed. "But as for the things you're talking about, that would come in handy but is not necessary. The missus and I, we've made do with less."

"I'm sure you have, but we want to do this." Judge Machel handed them a packet. "The other kids are at the hospital now, being checked over and made sure that nothing untoward has happened to them. After they're finished up there, there will be a couple of things they'll need to know and then you can take them over. It's a big responsibility, but I'm sure of all the people that have come through my courtroom, you two will do it best."

Christian left for home soon after the meeting ended. He was ready to take a couple of days off, hang around the house, and have some fun with his new bride. There was a lot going on right now, but he was sure that it wouldn't look so bad after some rest and relaxation.

~~~

Park hated to see Landon walking around like nothing had happened. Here he was, cooped up in a house without any food or running water, and there that man was running around town with the woman that Park hated almost as much as he did Landon.

Allie Stanton, as the papers were calling her now, seemed to have been given everything she would ever want on a silver platter, and the entire thing then dipped in gold. It pissed him off more than he'd been in a long time.

"Well, it's time that I did something about my situation." He had also began talking to himself more lately. Not that he thought anyone would give him good answers should there have been anyone around, but he was sure that he was smarter than the fucking cops. "Them not even looking in this building for me is about the stupidest thing I've ever come across."

Food was going to have to be his first priority. He was starving, and the small amount he could find in the vending machines he'd ripped off wasn't filling the void for him. Not even a little. And he was so sick of soft drinks that he would never have one again, he decided. There had to be more than sugary drinks offered in those things.

Sitting back down on the floor, he thought of what he had to do to make this work out for him. He needed money and to get out of town. Probably the country. It was bad enough that they'd caught him with the trumped up charges of murder, but now they'd add escaping from the prison to that. He was in a lose/lose situation.

A plan started to form in his head. He was going to kidnap Landon. Get him to sign something that stated that he was his heir and that Park would get the insurance money. He wasn't clear on the details on how that was supposed to work—collecting it would be a bitch—but he wasn't that far along in his plan just yet.

"Maybe he could go to the bank, bring it back to me, and I'd…. I'd what?" He closed his eyes, thinking of Landon just walking around, and grinned. "Or I could take that woman, Allie, and hold her until he returned with the cash. I'm gonna kill them both anyway, so why not get a two for one sale?"

The more he thought of his plan, the better he liked it. Allie would be gone and no longer a pain in his ass. And Landon would be dead as well. For the simple reason that in the last few months, years really, he'd been making things very difficult for him and his mom. Which brought up something else.

He'd have to get his mom out. Free her somehow. He didn't know how that would work. Landon would give him the money, but then how did he wait around for someone to come along and get his mom out for him? Contact would have to be made. And payments due. But as far as he could think, there just wasn't any way for him to do anything for her. She was going to have to be on her own.

"She always lands on her feet. Never seen a person that could do that better than my mom."

She did too. Whenever they needed some cash or a place to stay, his mom would come through for them. Money? Mom could sucker some rich fuck to hand it over to her without any questions. A place to stay? Hotel rooms were set up, food was brought to them, and there was even a little extra for her should she find herself in need of some company for the night. His mom was the best there was at providing.

"Nothing like Landon." He had forked over some heavy cash for him when his mom had first come to marry him. Twice he'd bailed him out. Park was sure that it mostly had to do with his mom making sure that it happened. But it did, and that was all that had mattered at the time. But then lately, since he'd been in prison, Landon had gotten dumber. Or smarter. However one wanted to look at it.

Park hadn't been too upset that his cards had been cut off. His mom had always come through for him in that area too. She'd charge up a bunch of crap that she knew she'd never wear and then take it back to the store a couple of weeks later for the cash. Landon thought that she was spending all his money, when in actuality, she was robbing the man. And then giving half of it to Park.

Even shopping trips with her friends had only been him

and her. They saw plays, went to the best restaurants, as well as bought clothing and other things to make them happy. His mom's motto had been, "You can't take it with you, so spend someone else's while you're still kicking."

As he worked through the details of his plan, he kept coming back to the fact that his mom would have to face things on her own. He hated to do that to her. But he also knew that she'd want the best for him. And she'd take this hit just to save his ass. It was what he'd do for her if they were in different roles.

"Mom is the best." He believed that too. There wasn't anything he couldn't ask for from her, and nothing she'd not give him. They were tight. "So, I'm just doing what she'd want me to do."

By morning Park had a plan. He was going to get the two of them, Landon and Allie, and tie them up in this building. To his way of thinking it was the perfect place. Not even the cops had been here once to find him.

He didn't have anything to restrain them with, so that was going to be a problem, but he figured that knocking them on the head once would subdue them enough. He knew for a fact that Allie was a fighter. He had enjoyed that the most in their time together. And while he was at it, he might remind her what it was like to have someone like him between her legs.

"Yes, sir, this might be a bigger payoff than I thought at first. Money, pussy, and a way out of town."

But Park did search the entire building for anything he could use to tie them with. Luck was on his side, and he thought of it as an omen that not only did he find a large thing of rope, but someone had stashed a little fridge in the sublevels with some food in it. He did wonder how he'd missed that before, but had a nice dinner of a sandwich with extra meat on it, as well as a couple bottles of water. After that, he went up to the top level again and had a nap. He wanted to be his best when he went after Landon and Allie.

He knew their routine now like he did his own. They would stop at the hardware store, spend about ten minutes there, and then move onto the little shop across the street. He had wondered why they would zigzag back and forth between the stores, but thought it was the mind of the rich and stupid and didn't give it too much more thought. Then they'd meet one or more of the Stanton men.

He knew who they were now. All of them. Big men with no necks that he'd bet lifted cars as a way to keep their bodies toned. Or they were on drugs. He was beginning to think it was the latter of the two, because they were forever being saps around any woman they were around.

The married one…he didn't know their names, but he was married to this woman who looked butch. He thought at first she was one of the brothers, but he realized his mistake when he saw her in a skirt and blouse. There wasn't any mistaking her for anything but a broad.

Each of them would fall all over themselves trying to open doors for one of them. Or walking with their hands tight in their own. And the elder woman, he thought it was their mom, she seemed to run the entire family like a harpy. He'd not actually seen her harp on them, but there wasn't any other reason for them to treat her like a queen except that she demanded it.

"Tomorrow is the big day." Park was ready. He was going to get them when they came out of the hardware store and before they went to the deli for lunch. Or he thought, he'd get them after and then he'd have their food they usually took to the park to eat. "Might as well have a nice meal while I'm at it."

Chapter 11

Christian moved through the tall grass quietly. Allie could see him, could even smell him, but she was careful where she stepped. One break of a twig and she'd be found. Waiting until he moved downwind of her again, she slid out from behind the dead tree and to the creek not far from her. The ability to shift into anything had a great many advantages.

I know that you're close and more than likely watching me, but I give up. What are you and where are you? She stood up as herself. *I walked right by you. Damn, but you're good at this. Are you ready for me to try?*

"Yes, I told you before I came out here we needed to try." She told him she'd been a snake. "They're harder to be, just so you know. All I want to do is eat things that are smaller than me. And mice. Gross."

Yes, I can see where that would be a problem. We'll have to remember to eat dinner before we come out to play. He shifted, then shifted back and he looked shocked. "I guess this is going to work. I've never been able to have clothing before. I just assumed that I'd left them behind."

"I like it. I mean, just as Dane said, it's much easier to be something in a hurry if you don't have to worry about what to wear when you're safe." He nodded. "Are you really ready? I'm to understand that Brayden hasn't even tried yet. He's being a chicken shit."

"I think he likes having the mystery of it all." Allie snorted. "Yeah, that's what I thought too. He's a big baby. All right, I'm ready. What is the easiest thing you've done?"

"All of them." He nodded and looked around. Then before she could tell him to hurry up with it, he was a great falcon. "You're beautiful. Can you fly?"

The skies seemed to have opened for him. A ray of bright sunlight opened above him and he took off toward the opening. As soon as he was out of sight, she did the same, shifting into a falcon to join him. Allie loved to fly.

Freedom. It was all she could feel when she took to the skies. And when she found Christian, she thought that he might be having as much fun as she was, just taking his time riding on the wind currents.

I can see for miles. Laughter rang in her ears as he continued. *I've never.... Even in a plane, I don't have as much freedom as I do right now. How do you ever come back from this?*

It's not hard when I know that you're there waiting for me. He flew by her, clipping her wing as he did so. *I love you, Christian.*

And I you, my love.

They flew around for nearly an hour, just dodging in and out of currents, landing on tree branches when they were tired. And when they returned to their home, just after dark, they walked hand in hand to the house and were greeted by her dad.

"Hello, sweet. I have something I'd like to talk to you

about. Both of you." They sat on the deck and Allie thought this was serious. Her dad rarely spoke to her without Mom around. "I'm going to ask you for money, but you're not to feel like you have to lend it to me if you don't want to. I have me an idea, and I'd like to get some startup money."

"What's the idea? And so you know, I'd have no problem telling anyone *no* if I didn't think it was a good idea. But with you, I have a feeling that you've been thinking on this for a long time." Dad nodded at Christian. "Go ahead, pitch me your idea."

"As you know, I don't have any legs." Her dad flushed. "I'm not doing this well. I'm better at blurting, as my wife calls it. So, if you don't mind, I'll do this my way instead of the way that Allison told me to do it."

"I'd like that. And while we're on the subject, I have been doing a little investigating on your accident. They're negligent on their part, and I'm suing them for compensation." The look on her dad's face looked just like she felt. Shocked. "They've done this before. Had someone get hurt and then not pay anything for the damages or medical that was done. I'm going to win this one, and when I do, I'm going to make sure that you're well compensated for this."

"That's...I was going to say that's not necessary, but I'm thinking that it is. Allison and I have been running for the last few years, as I'm sure you've figured out." They both nodded at her dad. "Well, I'm wanting to say that we had no choice, but the truth of the matter is, we just didn't want to face yet another bad thing. When we were running we were sort of free, but it's getting to be too much for us. Mostly for Allison, since she had to do most of the work."

"I understand. And I want you to know that the house that you and Allison found is paid for. Taxes too. Like Allie said, we want you to hang around for a little while. Forever if you'll be able to stand us." Dad nodded and wiped at his face, a sure sign that he was overwhelmed by it all. "Now that we have that settled, what is this idea you have? I'm all for anything new and exciting."

"I can't get around like other people. I mean, there are some exercise equipment things that I can use, but a lot of them I can't. And getting in and out of them places is hard on a family. They have wheelchair access, but there isn't any real access for us once we're inside. Like the weight machines? They have those for people that can get around, putting on the weights and all, but not for someone like me. And while we can get some help, it sure does put us in a bind when we don't have anyone to help us getting help with spotters and all." Christian nodded and pulled out his little notebook. As her dad spoke, Christian wrote things down. "Showers are all right too, but again, things aren't easy. There are some of us injured people that can't turn the water on and off. Also, sometimes it would be nice if we could have a chair, dedicated just for men and women like me that can't get their own wet."

"This is an excellent idea. And we could add in trainers too. Ones that have the same experiences that you have noted. I can see this being a big hit, Heath. I mean, the veterans in town alone will benefit from this a great deal." Her dad suggested that they start small. "No, I think we should start big. And we'll have a medical staff on hand as well. Physical as well as mental help. I love this. You've come up with an idea that is going to benefit a great many people with little cost to anyone other than a building, which I have the perfect one in mind. My dad could help with the medical, and I'm sure that some of his old cronies could come in and help out with everything else."

Allie went into the house while the men talked. She heard them come in an hour later, but they had made their way to the office rather than to bed. Smiling at her mom when she joined her in the living room, she told her what was going on.

"Your dad had been talking about this for weeks now, since we stopped at a camp ground that had some equipment that he wanted to try out. He was complaining that he was putting on some weight." Allie asked her if they were all right with moving into the house. "Yes. More than I thought we would be. And with the house set up for Heath, we're going to be able to stay there longer than we would have anything we could have afforded. I'm going to pay the two of you back for this."

"You want to pay me back, then you and Dad stay here and babysit for us once in a while." Her mom nodded. "I'm glad that you're here. Perry found a place as well. A house this time. He said it was time he started dating again too."

"I've been worried about him. Not you, never you. You have something in you that makes you have to bounce back, no matter what has gotten you down. But not Perry. He's.... Well, he's more delicate, I think. Your dad and I think that's what made him go into this type of business. He needed to prove himself." She could see that, but asked her mom why she did what she did. "You needed to prove to yourself that you were stronger than whatever was hurting you on the inside. That man, he took a great deal from you, but you, I think, got more back when you started to heal. Not just physically, but mentally as well. You are stronger of mind and body."

"I feel stronger too. And now that I have Christian in my life, I feel like I could take on the world. I won't, but I feel good." Mom leaned back on the couch. "I'm going to defeat Park. Dane and I, we're going to make sure that he doesn't hurt anyone again."

"I have no doubt that you will. And as much as I'd like to beg you not to do this, nor to get hurt, I know that you have to. It's something that will make you end it all. Do you still have nightmares?" She had to think about it. And when she told her mom no, not since meeting Christian, Mom laughed. "Yes, I figured he was keeping you much too busy to worry about bad dreams. I like the young man, and can't think of a better one than him that you should have married. You did well, my dear."

"Thanks. I think you're right."

They talked for a bit more, mostly about the upcoming holiday. She'd never been a big fan of the holidays, but she had a feeling that this year and for the rest of her life might be different. Having family and friends around would be a big undertaking, but it was something to look forward to as well.

At midnight, she made her way up to bed. Christian was still in his office; Dad had gone to bed not long before she had. As she stretched out on the bed, she heard Christian coming up the stairs and her body warmed at the sound. When he opened the door, he let his cat take him as he made his way to her.

~~~

He wants you. Allie nodded and sat on the edge of the bed. *There are two things you should know before I take you. One, you're beautiful and I love you.*

"That's two things." He told her it was. "And the second thing? If you're going to tell me that you're no longer in love with me, I won't believe you."

Never that. No, not ever that. You're in heat. She asked him what that meant. *You and I could make a child should you want.*

"Don't you have any say in this?" Christian told her that

it was her body. "No, sorry, but the moment that you and I came together, everything I have is yours, including my body. Do you want children?"

Yes. Very much so. She nodded. *Do you? I mean, even if you didn't want to have them now, I'd like to know that. I don't want you to feel you have to do anything this life changing just because you're a cougar now.*

"And I wouldn't. But to have your child, have a baby by you, with you, would give me the greatest joy on earth." Christian thought about shifting again, taking her as her husband, but his cat was a little antsy and had been all day. He knew why now, but to shift now would piss him off. "Do we have to tell anyone? Or will they know as soon as we conceive?"

No one will know unless we tell them. Not your parents either, of course. Allie stood up and pulled her nightgown off. When it dropped to the floor, his cat growled low and moved toward her. *He's very happy with you. Just in case you didn't know that.*

"I can tell. He eats me like I'm all he ever wants to fill his belly." The cat nudged her back to the bed and she did as he wanted. "Oh, Christian, I cannot wait to have you inside of me."

Christian couldn't taste her when his cat had her. He knew the excitement, the fulfillment of it, but not her taste. He wanted it, more than he did to hear her scream out his name, but his cat needed to have his fill of her as well, especially now that they were both aware of her being ready to give them a cub.

Allie gave as much as he took from her. Her cream and love made them both feel as if they were all she needed. She was certainly more than they could have asked for in a mate. Strong and willing, smart and articulate. He loved her. And so did his cat.

When he'd had his fill, he left her on the bed. Allie didn't move…he'd given her so much pleasure that he knew that she was weak with it. So when Christian took his body back, stripping down while she watched him, he thought of all the things he wanted to do to her. And would too.

"I thought about taking you hard, leaving you in a puddle of human flesh after I was done." She asked him what had changed his mind. "You did. I want to take you gently. Make love to you softly, and hear your breathless screams flow over your lips."

"You're so romantic. I love you for that." He lay down beside her on the bed, holding her hands above her head then settled over her. "You are the most wonderful thing that has ever happened to me. I love you."

"And I love you." Christian slid inside of her, his cock stretching more as he filled her. "You fit me. You fill me too."

They made love without words. He laved her skin with his tongue, loving the way she tasted to him. Touching her with his free hand, he could feel each muscle, every quiver of her skin. It was like heaven and hell to him. To have all this beauty and no words to tell her what she meant to him.

Pulling her hand free, she touched him as well. Her fingers caressed his back, tightened around his muscles. Everywhere she touched him, his skin burned for more. She was his, he kept telling himself, forever and beyond.

"I love you." He kissed her and then rested his forehead on hers as he continued. "You are all I ever wanted in my life. I might not have shown you that at first, but you are. Forever."

"I love you as well. Christian, give me a child, please."

He took her harder then. His body needed to fill her

with his seed. The thought of her heavy with child, her body carrying someone, a person that was a part of them, made his head spin and his body quake with happiness. As his climax reached peak, his body bowed up and he threw back his head. Emptying into her, his body and hers making another human being, was the most epic thing that he could have ever done.

She came with him, her cries of release bouncing off the walls and into his heart. Christian took her again, leading her up over the mountain and dropping her over the cliff. As she came a third time, holding him as she too bowed up off the bed, Christian leaned down and bit deeply into her throat, feeling her blood fill not only his mouth but his entire being as well. Christian had a mate, and she loved him.

When he woke, he was alone in the bed. The sun wasn't up yet, not as far as he could tell, but when he reached out to Allie to see where she was, he smiled when she told him to wait. Something had her upset, but he was sure that she could handle it.

Getting out of the shower, he dressed in his new jeans and T-shirt. They felt a little strange after wearing a suit most of the time, but he didn't mind them. As he made his way down the stairs, he could hear shouting in the kitchen and made his way there. He was surprised to see his brother, Colton, sitting at the kitchen table, being yelled at by Allie.

Not saying a word, he took the plate of food from Mrs. Apple and sat at the same table. Allie was on a roll and he let her go. It wasn't about him, so he figured that he'd stay out of it. And it worked until Colton said his piece.

"I didn't mean to upset you, Allie. That wasn't my intention when I came here." Christian asked his brother what was going on. "I have decided to give up my practice."

She hit Colton on the back of the head when he spoke.

"I take it she's not taking it all that well?" Colton grinned and snatched a piece of bacon off his plate. "What are you planning to do?"

"I'm glad you asked." Allie huffed at them both before leaving the kitchen. Colton asked for breakfast of his own and Winston nodded. "I'm going to run the veteran's place you and Heath are putting together. Well, not run it so much as work there. For free. I need a break."

"And that has Allie upset, why?" He told him. "Ah. Well, she has been working hard all her life just to make ends meet. I can see where she'd be upset with you for quitting a paying job. But did you explain to her that you, like us, don't need to work?"

"Nah, it was much more fun to hear her care so much about me than to burst her bubble of anger. She sure can be pissy when she wants." Colton got up and came back to the table and handed him what looked like a contract. "I want you to look this over for me. It's pretty standard if you ask me, but I'm not good at these sorts of things like you are."

Christian looked over the first few pages, then laid it aside in favor of talking to his brother and eating. He remembered how much energy he'd burned up last night, and thought that he could make that a nightly thing if Allie was willing. Taking a bite of his eggs, he talked around his food.

"You're selling your practice, not just leaving it?" He said it was easier than just having the other doctors that he worked with find another place. "I think that's a good idea. I'm assuming that Allie didn't know about this either."

"Nope. Did you know that you get all sorts of tax breaks for making this work? I'd not take too much of them, if I were you. Because once you do, you open the door to all sorts of agencies that want to rule it for you. There will be rules, I know, but I can help you with those as well." Christian told him he'd appreciate the help. "And you should also know, just so when you see it in there. I've put it in the selling contract you have that the doctors from the firm I had will volunteer once a month or more. I suppose, depending on the need at the clinic, that you're going to have one there as well."

"We don't even have it all together yet and you're willing to help us? Why?" Colton didn't answer but continued to eat. "Colton, why are you avoiding this?"

"I'm burned out. I mean, I love what I do and it's very rewarding, but I really just need a break." He asked him what was going to happen when he grew tired of helping out the other men. "I don't think it will. Not for a while anyway because I have a desire to write a book. On mental health. Not self-help, but an actual book about what I've come across that works, as well as things that didn't work out the way I had planned. And to get an insider voice for what really happens when someone suffers. Like these men and women do. I mean, it's not just mental for them, but physical and social too. How they're dealing with it and some of what they'd like to have changed. Not that I can change a great deal, but I can put the word out there."

"I think you'd be good at this." Colton thanked him. "But you have to talk to Allie. I don't want her upset. Not right now."

"She's in heat." He nodded and told him they were going to have a baby if they could. "I'm so happy for you both, Christian. It'll be nice to have little ones around here. I cannot wait to be an uncle. I think Dane and Brayden are waiting for her to go into heat again too. We'll be a huge family in a few years."

"You think she's out there for you? Your mate, I mean."

155

Colton said he wasn't sure if there was anyone for him, that his chance was gone. "You don't know that, Colton. You can't know that."

"I can't have children, Christian. We all know that. Whoever I brought into my life, if there is someone out there, they'd have to know that and be able to deal with it. The accident I was in as a teenager took all that from me." Christian said nothing but watched Colton finish his breakfast. "But on a better note, I have to go and talk to Mom and Dad about what I've done. In the event that Allie hasn't gone to tell them. If so, I'm guessing that the back of my head will need some padding by the end of the day."

Colton left right after that. Winston sat down across from him and he waited. The man hadn't been with him long, but their relationship, no matter how new, seemed to span lifetimes. Finally, Christian asked him what was on his mind.

"The LaRues. Do you think they'll need a cook or someone that can be there for them?" He asked him what he meant, telling him that the cook they'd had in mind bailed on them. "Well, I know that the mister is hurt and can't get around as well as the others. And the missus, she needs, if you don't mind me saying so, someone to take her out and have some fun. Both of them, as a matter of fact. And I have in mind someone that can go in and shake things up for them a bit."

"Your mate?" He nodded. "What does Daniel think about you getting a job for him? I mean, he is pretty touchy about things at times."

"He is the one that suggested it. Since his restaurant days are over, he's been moping about the house. I haven't said anything to him, thinking that he needed some time, but he came to me just yesterday and asked me to find out. With things so busy around here, I forgot until today. What do you think?" Daniel could shake things up a little for the couple, but he wasn't sure of their views on homosexuality. "They've met him, if that's what you're wondering. And anyone that meets him, they know that he's not straight."

"Yes, that is true." They both laughed. "And this meeting, was it your idea or his? I don't want them ambushed."

"Oh no, nothing like that. He was in the grocery store the other day and they were as well. Allison was having some trouble getting the wheelchair out of the car, and Daniel helped them. Then he spent the next couple of hours with them, having the time of his life, he told me." Christian asked how that had gone. "Well, he said that he helped Allison fix dinner for them, and then they sat around and enjoyed some show on television while Heath went on and on about how fine it was to have someone help in the kitchen and how delicious things were. I know that's not a glowing recommendation, but they know that he's my other half."

"You'd have to have him talk to them. I mean, be on the up and up about why he's not working in the food industry any longer. They might understand about the two of you, but attempting suicide might be a bit much for them. And they might worry about his state of mind." Winston said that he understood that. "Well, if he was asking for permission from me to do this, then I don't think you needed it so much as you wanted it, right?"

"Yes. I love Daniel, very much, but it worries me to no end when he is like he has been of late. I honestly think that being with the LaRues will help him in more ways than anyone could imagine. And I've talked to Colton as well. He said that getting out and back on the horse, so to speak, will be the best thing for him." Christian could see that and told Winston he agreed. "Good. Thank you. I'll talk to him today and tell him to go see them."

Christian went to his office. He didn't have much on his plate today, but he did want to finish up some paperwork. He also had to go over the contract that Brayden had given him for a new design on something, as well as Colton's paperwork. Today was going to be a long one, he thought.

Chapter 12

Joy was pacing in her cell. She hated being there, but no amount of talking to anyone would get her out. The door opened at the end of the hall, but she didn't care. It wasn't lunch time, the only way she had to tell time, nor did anyone come to see her. When she heard her name, she looked at Landon.

"What are you doing to get me out of here?" He didn't answer her and that pissed her off. "Landon, I've been in here a month now, and you've not come to see me once. Don't you love me anymore?"

"No, I don't think I ever did, if you want to know the truth. And you've not been in here a month, Joy. It's only been four days. I've come to give you some information, and what you do with it, it's up to you." She asked him if it had anything to do with her getting out of there. "No, nothing at all. Just information."

"I can't believe you're doing this to me. Is it because of the money I spent? I told you when I agreed to marry you that I had a habit of shopping. You assured me that you had plenty of money to let me have fun." He opened a chair and sat down while she continued. "Then you cut me off, and my son. That isn't what we agreed on."

"No, it's not. And that is my fault. But you didn't just spend my money, did you, Joy? You warmed my bed with countless other men. Stole things from my home and gave them to Park. Even after I forbade you to give him anything, you did that as well." She pointed out that he was her son. "Yes, but he's a grown man and should be making it on his own now. Not coming to me like a teenager for every little thing. Not to mention, he should have been in prison a good deal longer than he was, instead of you getting him out."

"I needed my little boy." Landon said nothing again. "Why are you here? To rub it in my face that you're thinking of divorcing me?"

"I have divorced you, Joy. It's a done deal. No, what I'm here for is to tell you that you're not getting out. They've found enough information on the murder of your first husband to know that you were aware of how he was killed." She didn't say a word, knowing that he was either recording her or someone was. "I want to offer you my help."

"Oh, thank goodness. I knew that you'd not be able to live without me. When are you getting me out of here? I have to make some sort of arrangement about Park too. You know that my son is innocent of all these things that are being said about him." She waited on him to say something. "You are going to get me out of here, aren't you? I mean, you said you'd help me."

"I did, but I'm not getting you out. I was thinking more along the lines of helping you out when you got to prison." She said it was harder to get out once you were there. "Yes, you'd know that as well, wouldn't you? What I mean is, I'll make sure that you have money in your account while there. It won't be as much as you want, I'm sure, but it'll be—"

"Money in my account? How is that going to help me, Landon? I'm your wife, not some prostitute that you took to your bed." He said there wasn't much difference as far as he could see with her. "What is that supposed to mean?"

"You had sex with me when it benefited you. And when it didn't, you would find someone else to give you what you needed. I would—and this was known to me from the very beginning—have sex with you, then have to pay out the ass for something you wanted. That might not be what you were, a prostitute…perhaps I should have said whore." She wanted him to come closer so that she could slap him, something that she'd been known to do when she was pissed off. "You're positively green right now. Something not agreeing with you, Joy?"

"You mother fucker. You knew that I had certain tastes when you married me. What sort of fucker gives and gives then takes away?" He asked her if she was referring to him or her. "You, you damned asshole. I want you to get me out of here. Right fucking now, Landon, or so help me, you'll regret it." He stood up and she watched him carefully.

Landon didn't have a temper as far as she knew. He would get angry, but he never screamed and yelled about it. He would get you in sly, devious ways. Ways that you'd never see coming until it was much too late to prepare for it. Like this divorce that he had done without her knowledge. Taking her money from her and leaving her son out to dry.

"I guess you've answered my question." He turned to leave, just picked up the chair, folded it, and put it back against the wall where it had been. "Have a nice life, Joy. I know that I will from now on."

161

"Wait. Come back here, Landon. I think you forgot something. When are you getting me out of here? This is not a place where your wife should be." He told her that he was no longer her husband. "Whatever you say. But I know as well as you do that you can't just abandon me here. You have to have some feelings for me. Enough that you came here to see me. Please, I don't want to be here anymore."

"I do have feelings for you. Contempt. Confusion. I even have some awe of you, but not in a good way. Mostly that I cannot believe that I didn't see through you sooner."

She started screaming at him then, to let her out of there.

When he was gone, she stood there calling his name for ten minutes, waiting for him to return. It would be just like him to make her do this and he'd go on home. There wasn't any way that he was going to leave her here. He needed her.

Finally sitting down, she thought of the conversation that he'd had with her. Most of it was bullshit, she knew. Yes, she had had something to do with Victor being dead, but Park had done it, poisoning him over the course of a few weeks. She had only bought it for him, she'd never fed it to her late husband.

Where was Park? She knew that he had escaped from jail. How was a mystery to her, but she knew that he was out. The dumb fuckers here wouldn't tell her much, but she was happy that he was out enjoying himself. She just hoped that he'd not forget about her.

When he'd been about ten the two of them were on their own. Park had been very resourceful in his youth. They were never hungry so long as he could do his thing, and for a very long time, there was always money coming in. Joy never asked. She thought it best not to know too many details about what he did to get cash. Then, about fifteen years later, he told her about Landon and his millions. He'd even made it so that she could dress the part of a widow, and told her not to mention Park too much.

"He might not like that you're old enough to have a son my age." She asked him why not. "Because men like Landon Hartman like to have young pretty things on their arm, not someone that has a son old enough to vote."

He'd been wrong about that. Landon had known how old she was, as well as about Park. She hadn't been happy about it, that he'd done a search on her, but since he didn't seem to mind, she'd brought Park to their home and given him free run of whatever there was for the two of them. In fact, they had more fun when Landon was away than they did when he was there. But things got complicated.

Park had always been a very rambunctious boy. And as he grew into adulthood, his way of making people do for him had gotten violent. Joy had tried, a great deal over the years, to tell everyone to just let him have his way and things would go better for them, but no one wanted to listen. Then that woman had come along and told those horrible lies about him.

Like he'd been able to be that sadistic. It wasn't possible. Yes, he did have tastes about sex that scared her a great deal, but he'd never hurt anyone in the process. Those women, she knew, had led him on because they thought he had money. Which even back then, when one of the women had said he'd taken her, they'd only had the appearance of having it, but never really had anything but barely a pot to piss in.

Landon had been no help when she wanted Park released. He told her that he had to pay for his crimes. As far as she knew the only crime he had ever committed was wanting more than he had. That was no reason for him to be in trouble all the time. Those women that had come forward, they had somehow gotten it into their heads that he was a bad man. When he was just her little boy.

Then there was the last murder. If she told him once, she'd told him a million times, never get caught at what you enjoy. Of course, he never listened to her. Not any time she'd had to go and bail him out of trouble. But the murder of the drug dealer had been recorded, and it was hard to hide that.

"What's a mom to do? I've been taking care of him the best I could all these years, and I've failed him. Just failed him when he needed me the most." She cried as she sat there, wondering what she could have done differently to make him a better man. "Money would have helped, and stability. Lord knows I tried to make his life stable by being with men that had money."

She'd been married four times trying to help her son. Divorce had been a tricky thing to get finalized. Only with Landon had she had to sign a prenup. But he had been the biggest catch of all, and she believed she could get around that. Apparently, she thought, she was losing her touch. Oh, if only Park were here with her.

He'd been such a wonderful little boy, always trying new things, getting into little spats with the other children in the neighborhood. Other parents had restrictions on their children as far as she was concerned, stifling their creativity and their minds. Sometimes it would be days before he'd return home, always calling her to let her know that he was busy and not able to come back right away. So long as she knew that he was safe, Joy never had a problem with his adventures.

Even when he'd been in trouble with the police, she'd not worried about him. He had a quick wit and ability to get himself, and admittedly her as well, out of jams quite easily. And as he got bigger and stronger, he was even more helpful to her. Like when she would go on dates.

She supposed some people would look at it as something wrong, rolling men for their cash and jewelry. But to her, and to Park, it was a way to survive. The dates would take her to a nice dinner, where she would flirt and come on to them. Then a few minutes after they'd get to the hotel or even a parking lot, Park would come and help her out of it. The men, they were such fools when it came to fighting Park. No one ever won against his amazing strength and agility.

"I miss you, my son." She lay down on the cot, her eyes watery thinking about how long it had been since she'd held him. Hugged him to her. "Be safe. That's all I ever wanted for you."

~~~

The courtroom was filled to capacity. Allie and Perry sat with their parents, and Christian's parents sat with them as well. It was a full row of people, with his brothers all leaning against walls when seating became hard to find. Her dad wasn't thrilled about being there; he was glad that Christian had done this for them, but he didn't like being in the public eye.

"All rise." Everyone stood but her dad, but he did sit up straighter in his wheelchair. When they were seated again, the judge asked to see both attorneys in his chambers. Within minutes both the representative from the company that her dad had worked for as well as Christian were led to the double doors.

"Do you know what's going on?" She shook her head at her mom. "This is all so strange. Don't you think? To get us all here then tell us to wait. I hope that Christian isn't in trouble about this."

"He's not. I'm sure."

When Allie reached him, he asked her to wait. He needed to pay attention. But it didn't make her worry any less. After about an hour, they were told there was going to be a break, and that everyone should return in two hours. Allie and her family, along with the Stantons and Landon, made their way to the deli across the street.

She saw Park out of the corner of her eye. Dane told her to sit still, and in a few minutes, she was told to go to the ladies' room with her. The two of them stood up and made their way there just as Landon moved to the men's room. In seconds she and Dane were ready.

"Now remember, don't engage him unless he does us first." Allie nodded. "You look amazing. And you've studied everything, correct? You know the plan?"

"Yes, I can recite it in my sleep." Nodding, Dane left the ladies room first, then she followed. They were going to meet up outside the deli and wait. Brayden was going to be close but not seen. "Be careful."

Almost as soon as they started down the little street, Park came up behind them. They knew that he was unarmed, as they'd been really careful about watching his every move. Not to mention, the food he was eating was drugged, and he was sleeping like a baby when they went to check on him. The Feds had been very helpful in making sure the cameras were set up nicely as well. Everything he did was with all eyes on him.

"Come with me and no one has to die today." She started to turn, but he hit her with something. "I didn't say you could turn, Landon. When will you ever learn that I'm in charge?"

They walked where he told them to. The building was looming before them, and she could see men standing in the windows waiting for them. It would be over soon, and she

166

was glad for it. Remembering her lines when Dane nudged her, she spoke.

"Never. You're in deep shit if you think this is going to go in your favor, Park." She had to smile when Dane, as her, whimpered a little. "Don't you hurt her any more than you already have, Park. I won't have it."

"You won't have it? Well, that really makes me quake in my boots." She looked down at his slippered feet. The pop to the back of her head hurt, but she did catch her laughter. "This is the fault of the two of you. I'm going to get money and you're going to help me."

"No, I'm not." She was shoved into the building that he'd been staying in for the last few days. "What makes you think I'm going to help you anymore now than I did before?"

"I have a gun." She told him, sounding like Landon as best she could, that he didn't. "How the fuck do you know? I'm well-armed and dangerous."

"I see." He told her to tie up Allie, and for a second she was confused. But "Allie" putting out her hands had her doing what he wanted. "What do you suppose you're going to do now that you've taken us against our will? You think this is going to go anywhere but down?"

"I have the upper hand." When she was finished tying her up, Dane told her to be careful. Park told her that they were going to the bank. "You're going to clean out your accounts, then you're going to come back here and sit like I tell you, and you might live another day."

"I think you have plans to kill us both." Park laughed. "You going to just leave the country, Park? Leave your mother here to rot in a jail cell? Not very good of you, is it? But then, you've always been a selfish little prick."

He smacked her then, hard across the face, and she

167

wanted to curl into herself and let him hit her all he wanted. Memories and nightmares seemed to swamp her until she couldn't breathe around them. Then she felt him, heard Christian saying her name softly over and over.

It's all right baby. I'm here for you. You're doing fine. She sat up and looked around, her body hurting for what he'd done to her. Not just today, but before as well. *I'm right outside the building, baby. We're all waiting for you to go to the bank and then return.*

He wants me to take out all the money. He said he knew, he could see it. *I love you, Christian. So much. And when this is over, I want you to just hold me.*

I will. You do what he wants and we'll take care of the rest. I promise you, I'll be right there when this is done. She stood up and wiped the blood off her mouth with the dirty rag Park gave her. *You can do this, Allie. We're all right here waiting for you.*

The bank wasn't far, but she didn't want to leave Dane. She knew of all of them, she'd be fine, but she liked the other woman and worried all the same. When she entered the bank, she could see Julian at one of the teller windows, and Wyatt was sitting at the desk of a loan officer. She was sure there were more people in there to keep her safe, but she knew she was going to be just fine.

"I'm sorry, Mr. Hartman. But the bank can only give out ten thousand dollars every ten days to one person." He nodded, but whatever Park was poking into her back was painful. "You can take out more in ten days, with permission from the bank manager, but nothing today. I'm sorry."

"It's fine." But it wasn't, and Allie knew that Park wasn't happy. "Just give me what you can and I'll take care—"

"No, you'll get it all now." She was poked again. "Listen lady. I'm serious. I want you to empty my stepfather's account right now and give it all to me."

"I can't do that. I'm not going to be able to—"

The gun was fired over her head and Allie looked around the bank. He had a gun? He had a fucking gun?

"Now, do as I tell you, or I swear to Christ, the next bullet is going through your fucking empty head."

"You have a gun? Where the hell did you get a fucking gun?" Allie realized her mistake at once. She was no longer talking like Landon. "You weren't supposed to have a gun."

He aimed it at her head and she let go of Landon's form. Just as quickly, she shifted to her hawk and took off to the ceiling. In seconds he was firing at her until she heard the clicking of the gun. But before she could land to take him down, he was on the floor bleeding.

Allie stood back while the others did what they needed to take care of the incident. That's what they kept calling it, an incident. Like she'd not been shot at and Park wasn't dead.

"They didn't know about the gun." She looked at Dane and told her no shit. "They're still trying to figure out where he got it, but one thing is for sure, he got what he deserved."

"He did at that." She looked at the teller who had been shot as well. "She's going to be all right, isn't she? I mean, it's nothing more than a flesh wound, right?"

"Yes. She's going to be just fine. After she shifts, it'll be as if nothing happened." Christian hadn't been able to leave to be with her, so she sat still. "Allie, are you all right?"

"Yes. I mean, a part of me is appalled that I was a part of him being killed, but a bigger part of me is glad that he's gone and out of our lives. I would hate to have to tell Joy that her son is dead, however." Dane sat next to her. "Does the courtroom know what happened? I know that Christian does, but do the rest of them know?"

"No. And as you can imagine, Christian can't say anything. He'd be locked up if he told anyone what he knew. Instead he's still in the meeting with the judge." She nodded. "Are you mad at him for lying to you about being right there?"

"No. He calmed me, just what I needed for him to do." Dane sat down on the floor with her. "Your plan to switch ourselves around was wonderfully perfect. You saved a lot of lives with that."

"You did well too. Landon kept saying it was like looking in a mirror." Allie nodded. "The police are going over to talk to Joy now. I wondered if you'd like to take a flight with me. I need to get out and do something that doesn't involve death and maniacs."

Grinning, she nodded. She didn't wish for anyone to have been killed, but the thought of being in the sky with a friend made her laugh. Joy was going to be devastated—she would have been too had it been her own child—but she had raised him to be just what he was. A monster.

Chapter 13

The judge wasn't very happy. He had all kinds of files in front of him, and several more that looked like they'd been dumped and the paperwork just shoved back inside. They were in the hands of his secretary, who didn't look any happier than Judge Winshaw did.

Their meeting had been to go over offers from the company that owned the warehouse where Heath and the other men and women had worked. There were thirty-three different complaints against them, and not one of the people had ever gotten anything from the company. Now they were rushing to get things settled.

"This is an outrage." Christian said nothing. Judge Winshaw picked up the first folder. From where he sat, Christian had no idea whose name was on it, but he soon found out. "Peterson, David. Five hundred dollars. Shipley, Donna, four hundred dollars. You do know that these people were hurt, and the emergency room costs were much higher than this, don't you?"

"It's all my company can afford now, Your Honor. We

have tried to contact the injured before this, and none of them returned our calls." Winshaw asked for the names they'd called and when. "I'm not sure, sir. I've been told that we have tried. As the man who owns the company, I don't make calls, I order them done."

"I'm sure you do. And what do you think of these settlements? You think that they're even close to being a good closing amount?" The owner of the company, Vito Bolton, said it was fair. "Fair? You think that a man losing his home, his pension, as well as his life savings trying to pay for his wife's medical bills is fair?"

"I don't know what that has to do with the settlement, Your Honor. We have calculated the cost of the insurance that wouldn't pay for each incident, and that is the amount we came up with. So, yes, I think it's more than fair." Winshaw just huffed. "I have the checks made out for each of them. And paperwork for them to sign. If you'll just say that the case is settled, then we can—"

"You will not tell me how to run my courtroom, young man." Winshaw looked at Christian. "Is this the settlement you were hoping for?"

"No, sir, it is not. Add a few more zeros to each of them, then we'll be in the ballpark. But nothing like this." Winshaw nodded and looked at Bolton again. But Christian spoke first. "Sir, I have their financial records here, if you'd like to see them. Also for each of the victims that worked in the plant."

"How did you get those?" Christian said it was a matter of public record, and he'd just gone and asked for them. "Your Honor, whatever he has there, it's no proof that my company actually has that much money just lying around. We have investors that get paid, as well as other people that work for us. There isn't any way that we can pay out the sort of money that he wants for them anyway. It's just not going to happen."

Winshaw told Bolton to shut up. As the judge looked over the paperwork that Christian had given him, Christian asked Allie how she was doing. He laughed when she told him where she was headed.

I'm in the pocket of a man who is going to tell Joy about her son. I'm not sure that I want to see her grief, but this is an adventure. Not to mention, a very easy way to travel. Oh, and before you go home, you need to go and see Landon. He went home a little while ago, but I don't think he should be alone. This is hard on him. He said that he would. *My parents are going to your parents' house for a little while. My dad is having a hard time of this. This trial is bringing up memories and old pains, he said. Plus, he's sure that he's going to be in trouble. I told him that he was no longer in debt, thank you for that, but he is still afraid.*

I can well imagine. The hospital that he owed a great deal of money for is now a part of this case. They're suing the Bolton Holding company for billing too. It shouldn't be too hard on the company to pay up. They're worth just over three hundred billion dollars. She whistled and he laughed. *The judge is none too happy with the amounts they set up either. That's why this thing is taking so long. I'm hoping it'll be over soon. If not, then we'll be well into dinner soon.*

Dad and Mom just want to have their savings back. I don't blame them, but I'm hoping for more. My dad has suffered enough for this. Christian told her that everyone had. *I know that too. Well, we're about to enter the police station. I'll talk to you soon. I love you.*

I love you as well.

The judge cleared his throat and looked at them. Bolton was acting bored, but Christian could smell his fear. If things went as well as he hoped they would, a lot of people were going to be all right from now on.

"I have no idea why you didn't help these people when they asked for it. Firing them for getting hurt on the job is not just frowned upon, but it's also against the law. These people have suffered enough, as far as I can see." He lifted the files still on his desk and handed them out to Bolton. "You have an hour, and only that, to get me a better deal on the table for them, or I will do it myself. And let me tell you right now, I don't care if you must sell off your nice mansion to pay these people, you will do it."

"You can't expect me to just turn over the keys to my life. Do you have any idea how hard I've had to work to get to where I am today? Years and years." Winshaw said he'd done it on the backs of people who needed something too. "Then perhaps they should have gotten their shit together and gotten themselves a nice job as I have done. I employ two hundred people in my plant here alone. That is a lot of people to have on welfare if I were to close up and fire them all. If you make me do this, I might just do it anyway and no one gets a damned thing from me."

"Are you threatening me?" Bolton said nothing, but did shrug. "You little pisser. You just told me that if I don't do things your way, then you'll close up and have a great many people unemployed, didn't you?"

"I've made offers. If they don't want to take it, then that's their loss. If you come up with one cent more than is on those forms, then I'm closing my business and moving to a town that is much nicer about having their citizens employed." The judge looked at Christian, then back at Bolton as he continued. "That's my final offer. You do what you must."

The secretary that had been there the entire meeting left the room, only to return seconds later. She didn't say anything to any of them, but did hand Winshaw a sheet of paper. Again, Christian couldn't read what was on it, but a man in a suit came in just as Winshaw laid the paper down.

Judge Winshaw laughed. Christian wasn't sure what he found to be so funny, but he was careful not to get too overjoyed by it. Whatever was going on with the judge, Christian was sure that Bolton wasn't going to like it.

"Bolton, I'd like you to meet Monroe Sweet. And don't be fooled by his last name. He's a shark." Sweet laughed and pulled a pair of handcuffs from behind his back. "You and he have a great deal to talk about, it seems. And I'm going to go out to my courtroom in an hour and see what I can do for these poor folks."

"Vito Bolton, you are under arrest for attempting to bribe a county employee, threatening a sitting judge, tax evasion, as well as attempted murder on thirty-three people. You have the right—"

"What are you talking about? There is nothing you can arrest me on. I demand that you explain yourself." Sweet grinned and pulled out a file. He handed it to Christian. "Why is he getting it?"

"My hands are full at the moment, and I trust him a good deal more than I do you." Sweet nodded as he continued. "Go ahead, Dr. Stanton, read what's there for us."

Christian read over the first few lines. If even one of the things on this paperwork was true, the man was in deep shit. Sweet told him to read it please.

"You attempted to bribe a county employee who came to inspect your plant on each of the occasions that someone was hurt. You threatened another judge in another state for the same thing you mentioned here. Tax evasion? Well, it seems that the records that were found at your home an hour ago do not reflect what you turned in to the IRS." Christian looked at Judge Winshaw. "What does this do for the people I'm representing, sir?"

"They'll be paid out of the estate and moneys first. Then the government will take what they want. It should be a nice payoff for the injured." Christian read off the rest of Bolton's misdeeds.

As Bolton was being taken away, Judge Winshaw asked for two days to get things settled with the money. Christian said that it was fine with him. Then he was cautioned to keep things quiet. From everyone.

"I know that one of these people is your father-in-law. And I also understand that he's going to be asking you what happened. If you could just ask him to wait, I'll make sure that he's taken care of, all right?" Christian nodded. "Have you ever thought of running for judge? I think you'd make a fine one. A sitting judge means you could do much more."

"I never gave it any thought, sir. But I do like my life as it is now." Winshaw nodded, but didn't look convinced. "Really, I do like my life as a country lawyer."

"Yes, I'm sure you do. But think on it some. I'm ready to get out of this crap, and you'd be the perfect man to replace me. Like I said, think on it." Judge Winshaw stood up. "I'll contact you when I have these finished. You have a nice night, Christian. I know I will now."

Christian hadn't realized it had gotten to be so late. By the time he had gathered up his things it was close to five o'clock. Instead of reaching for Allie, he made his way to the station. He would be there for her if she needed him.

~~~

Allie could hear the men talking before she saw them. Christian was one of the men...the others, she didn't know.

But after she and Dane had come home, Allie had gone into town to be with him. When he saw her, he paused and put out his hand. She went to him and took it. The men shook his free hand before they peeled away from them.

"I'm going to go and see Joy with Landon. I guess she didn't take it well." Allie asked if he wanted her to wait. "No, I need you with me. I don't think that Landon is taking it well either. I know that he didn't like the man, but Joy was his wife and I think seeing her this way is going to hurt him."

Nodding, they made their way to the jail. Landon was there waiting on them, and she hugged him, telling him how sorry she was about his loss. He held her tightly, and she wasn't sure that he was going to be all right at all.

"He was a monster." She, wisely, said nothing. "To think that had I been there, if that had been me, he would have...I would be dead now if not for you. He didn't care about anyone but himself."

As they made their way through the maze of doors that led to the cells, she could hear Joy screaming. It was primal and from the heart. She didn't like either of them, Joy or Park, but to have your child killed would hurt anyone. As soon as Joy saw Landon, she started talking quickly and incoherently.

"They told me that he was dead. No, no, that's not right. They lied. No, he's not dead. My little boy would never try to kill anyone. Tell them, Landon. Tell them that he's not like that. I love him. This is a trick. They want me to hurt. No, I won't have it. Tell them, Landon. Tell them that they aren't to lie to me. That my baby boy is hiding out where the police won't find him. They never liked him. He's a good boy. Tell them." She started sobbing then, and Landon started forward and Joy spoke again. "Damn it, come here so that I can snap your fucking neck. This is all your fault, you know. You cut him off when he did nothing to warrant that. He's fine. I know it. Tell me that he's fine."

"He's dead, Joy." Landon took a step back, then another when Joy reached for him. He spoke to her calmly and quietly. "Park was killed when he tried to rob the bank. He shot another person before the security guard—"

"No, no, no, no. He's out there somewhere looking for me. Park would never do something like that. He wouldn't. Park was a good boy that no one understood." Landon looked at Allie and Christian; he was in pain too. "Landon, tell them to let me out. I need to go and find Park. I need for us to be together."

"I'm sorry, Joy, but that's not possible." Christian spoke to her in hard tones, but Allie knew what he was doing. He was trying to get her to see the reality of the situation. "Park was killed while robbing the bank, and he held Landon as hostage."

They had all agreed, with the way that things had gone down, that no one needed to know that she'd been in place of Landon. And the few that had seen her fly away, they weren't sure that's what they'd witnessed anyway, not with how things had happened. Allie was good with that. And Dane had agreed that she was also held as her, so that no one would dispute what really happened.

"Why are you doing this to me? Let me out, please. My little boy needs me. He's not dead." She looked at Allie. "This is all your fault. You did this to him when you lied on the stand. Why couldn't you have kept your mouth shut? Just what did you hope to gain by telling those lies about him?"

"Gain? I would guess that I gained my own freedom. And I didn't lie. He did those things to me and he enjoyed it." Joy called her a cunt. "No, I'm a survivor. And I will continue to be one too."

Joy paced the cell, walking back and forth the length of the small area, speaking to herself as well as in some cases, Park. She was devastated, and there was little to nothing that anyone could do for her. Not now. When she finally sat down, Landon stepped closer to the bars, but not close enough for her to touch him.

"He was all I had in the whole world, Landon. The only reason that I got up in the mornings, that I wanted to be alive." Landon said he was sorry. "Are you? Are you really? Because of you, I was in here and not out there helping him get what he needed. You cut us off and took away our fun. What did you expect him to do when you treated him this way?"

"Grow up. Find his own way to earn his keep. There are a lot of ways that he could have gotten what he needed to survive that didn't involve me supplying him with everything he wanted." She said it was his duty. "No, never my duty, Joy. Nor yours. He was a grown man that wanted everything given to him, and if not he took and took. That is no way to live."

"It was for him. It was for us." Landon told her again he was sorry. "You're not sorry enough, Landon. When I get out of here, and I will, you're going to be very sorry. See if you aren't. Park and I, we're going to take you for everything you have."

Landon hardened in that moment. Allie could see it on every line of his face...the carriage of his body, the way that he tightened his hands into fists. Anger blew off him in waves.

"I am sorry, Joy. Sorry that I ever met you. Sorry that I took on your son and let him walk all over me. But what I'm most sorry for is that you are sitting here in a jail cell, and more than likely will be for a very long time, and all you can

179

think about is how everyone around you hurt you. How it is everyone else's fault that your son is dead." He did step closer then and put his hands on the bars as he continued. "Have a wonderful life, Joy. I wish you all the best. But I'm sure that it will never be enough for you. I have made funeral arrangements for Park. He'll be buried in one week. You make your own arrangements to go or not."

He walked away then…through the door and out of sight. Joy sat there on the floor, rocking back and forth and smiling. Repeating over and over that Park was going to come for her at any time and that they'd all be sorry.

"We should go." She nodded at Christian, but stayed where she was. "Allie, what is it? She's not going to listen to you."

"No, I know that. But I don't think she needs to be alone right now." Joy kept rocking back and forth, talking incoherently now. "I'll be fine. Just go on to Landon. I won't get close to her."

He left her because she told him again she'd be fine. Sitting on the floor a few feet from the cell, she spoke quietly to Joy. She didn't know what to say to her about her son or what she'd done, so Allie spoke to her about things in her life.

"My father is a good man. A great one, to me anyway. My mom is the strongest person I know. I have a brother too." Joy continued to rock. "When I was a little girl, in fifth grade, my dad took me to the father-daughter dance. It was a special night for us."

Joy stopped rocking and stared at her. She didn't say anything, nor did she move, but watched her carefully. Allie started to smile, but was afraid that it would set her off for some reason.

"I had a lavender dress and he had a tie that matched

it. My mom curled my hair with clothespins. It seemed the strangest thing in the world to me, but it did look lovely when she took them out." Joy continued to stare, but she no longer looked vacant. "We went to the dance where all the other little girls and their dads were but for one girl. She was in my class, so I knew that her daddy had been killed. He was a police officer."

"I wanted to be one when I was a little girl. I thought it would be the best thing, to oversee criminals." Joy asked her why she'd not done it. "My dad told me that it was a man's job to care for the women, not the other way around."

"When I have a little girl, I'm going to teach her that she can be anything and everything she wants. The same for a son, should I have any." Joy nodded, but started rocking again. "So, I talked my dad into dancing the first one with Peggy. That was her name, Peggy White."

"She was lucky to have you as a friend." Allie nodded. "What will I do without my little boy? He was all I had in the world."

"I don't know, Joy. You can study if you want. I'm sure that there are all kinds of programs in—" Allie caught herself before mentioning the prison Joy would more than likely be going to in a few weeks. "You can do whatever you wish. Anything."

"I want to die. I don't want to live without my Park."

Allie wasn't sure she should say anything, and reached out to the only person she knew that would know what to say. Colton.

After telling him where she was and what she was doing, Colton asked her what Joy was doing. Allie told him what she'd done prior to her talking and what she was doing now. Still rocking.

You tell her that it was a great loss, but she has to move on for someone to know him. Tell his story. She said that she was going to prison. *Yes, she is, but they'll need to talk to her about her son. The relationship that she had with him, it was unhealthy for them both. It's good that they were close, but they were much too close.*

You mean they had sex? He said not that he was aware of, but that Joy saw Park as a child; he'd not grown up in her eyes. *But she could see that he was.*

Not to her heart. Allie told Joy what Colton said, and she could see the difference in her eyes. She had a purpose. A meaning. Telling the story of Park. *Come home, Allie. We're at your house and we need to be a family. It's been one hell of a day.*

"I have to go, Joy. Are you going to be okay?" Joy nodded and started rocking again. "All right. Tell them if you need something that we can get you, for them to call. Good night."

Allie went outside and let the cool night breeze flow over her. Christian was there with Landon, both sitting on the bench right outside the jail. Things were going to be hard on the older man, but she had a feeling that he was going to be all right now. If a little bruised around his heart.

Chapter 14

Christian was impressed that the land they bought was in such good shape. The mountaintop would need some work… trees planted and a few other plants that were needed to keep it from eroding away. But all in all, he was happy with their purchase. He looked at his dad when he came to stand next to him.

"There are several hundred volunteers down there that are ready to build some homes for them." Christian said that Brayden had called in some help and it was being taken care of. "I thought he was going to tell me no when I asked him to help, but he was right on it. I guess once a builder, always one."

"Food is coming in by plane in a few hours. There will be trucks too, but they're waiting on the temporary bridge to go up. Shouldn't be much longer with that. It's easy work since there was so much equipment left behind." Dad nodded. "Allie said that the doctors that you asked to come here are all working around the clock to make sure that everyone is healthy. One of the elders, a man that people said has been around forever, he wanted to talk to her so she's meeting with him and me in an hour."

"I met him too. Nice man. I think he has to be at least a hundred." Christian said he thought so as well. "I've been thinking a great deal about something. How you were with Allie when she first came to the family. Your cat, he was mean. Overly protective. Now, well, you seem to be all right with anyone being near her."

"Yes. I've noticed that as well. I feel calmer around the rest of them too. You think you know why?" Dad nodded as they made their way back down the long path that had been left by heavy equipment being moved. "Oh, before I forget, I wanted to tell you that we're having a baby in seven months. Allie is pregnant."

Dad stopped moving and turned to him. There was a look on his face, one that Christian hadn't ever seen before. He started to ask him about it when his dad spoke first.

"You sure?" He said that she'd gone to the doctor that morning so they could surprise everyone. "I thought...well, I had it in my head that she was. And my heart. But unlike other paranormals, we can't tell when one of our own is breeding. Heat, yes, but not when they conceive. I'm not sure what I should do."

"What do you mean?" Dad hugged him. Right there on the side of the mountain, he pulled him into his arms and held him tightly. "Well, this sure does seem the right thing to do."

"Your mom, she's gonna bust. You know that, don't you?" Dad let him go, then hugged him again. "I'm so excited. A baby. A grandchild. I just...."

After another hug, the two of them started down the path again. Christian was watching his footing, so he didn't see the large hawk that landed in front of them. As soon as Allie took her form back, Dad nearly tripped going to her and hugging her as well. They were both sobbing as he told her how much he loved her.

"I love you too. We were going to tell everyone tonight." Allie slapped Christian on the chest, then walked with them down the hill. "I have to go and meet Shalimar now. He was going to meet Christian and me both, but there's a phone call that Christian has to return."

"Who is it?" Allie said she didn't know, but that it was urgent. "I'll call them as soon as we get to the base, then join you."

There was no cell service yet. They were putting in cell towers now, but it would be a few more days before they were functioning. The company that had been here before had used walkie talkies to the base unit, who would make the necessary calls out. They, of course, had taken all that equipment with them when they were told to leave a month ago.

"All right." He asked his dad what he'd been about to tell him about his cat. "What's wrong with your cat?"

"Nothing at all. I was just telling Christian that I think I figured out what made him so mean when other people were around you. I think his cat knew that you'd been hurt and he wasn't able to protect you." Christian thought about that. Then his dad continued. "Then when you were converted, he was more relaxed because he knew that you'd been cured. And after Park was taken care of, everything went back to normal."

Christian made his way to the base and found his mom talking to Dane and a couple of the other women that were helping. Dane was making sure that things were safe for them all, and Mom was keeping them fed. Christian was looking forward to going home tomorrow and having Christmas in a few days. It had been a long month.

Picking up the note with the number on it, he called it. The service wasn't all that good, but he finally got through. The phone was answered by Allison, Allie's mom. She asked him to hold on, that Perry wanted to talk to him.

"Joy is dead." Christian sat down on the chair, thankful that it was close enough for him to fall into. "She hung herself this morning here, and they found her when they took her breakfast. She'd been dead for about six hours."

"Does Landon know?" Perry said that he did and was taking it better than expected. "He came to peace with it all, I think. What do you know so far?"

"Nothing much. She left a note. It was a little hard to understand from what I heard, but she basically wanted to see her son. Joy did mention Allie, saying that her coming to see her weekly was what kept her sane. But she was still in pain, and had waited until Allie was where you are before she killed herself." Christian watched his wife move across the road to the place where the people were being helped. "I thought you could let her know. Gently. She's going to take it pretty hard, I think."

"She will. Not that they were friends, I don't think, but she did want to help her some. And in a way, I think she did." Perry said it seemed like it. "I'll tell her tonight. We'll be leaving here in the morning. I hate to ask, but could you make arrangements for me?"

"I have already. Mom and Dad helped too. Oh, and you should know that they got the check today. My dad is about to bust a gut. He wasn't expecting nearly that much." Christian didn't know how much, so he asked him. "Four point three million dollars. And Mom got a check too, for compensation for being Dad's caregiver. They're actually looking at nice motor homes to go on short trips with."

Christian laughed. "Well, it'll have to be better than their old pop-up. And a good deal easier for them to set up." Perry said they were talking about how they could get it outfitted for Dad. "Well good for them. I'm really happy for them both."

He hung up a few minutes later and went to find Allie. She was sitting in an office alone, just staring at the walls, when he found her. Careful not to startle her, he asked her if she was all right.

"Yes. I just heard from Winston. He told me that Joy killed herself." Christian told her that he'd only just found out too. "He didn't want me to hear about it over the news reports. They said that she did it because I'd left. Not that I left her, but she waited until I was gone before she did it."

"Yes. She was in a bad way." She nodded, then climbed up into his lap like a small child. Christian put his hand over her tiny mound. "How's our little guy?"

"Ready to go home." He said he was as well. "I talked to Shalimar. He's a very nice man, did you know that? And he said that he can see into the future."

"Really? I did know that he was a nice man, but not the other." He held her, rocking just a little. "What did he want to talk to you about? Anything that I should know?"

"Yes, he said that he wanted me to have something. I have to go with him to pick it up in a little while. He was waiting on you." She stood up. "Let's go so that I can take you back to the hut and make love to you all night."

"Deal." They left the offices and Shalimar was on the path waiting for them. After she hugged the older gentleman, the three of them started walking. He spoke to them about things that he'd seen.

"Once, many years ago, there was nothing here but a man

and his goats. He would wander up and down that mountain like he was as surefooted as they were." Christian had seen a man with goats in town and wondered if it was the same family. "His goats would give the finest milk for cheese. When I was able to make it, people would come from miles to have a bit of it."

"I bet it was creamy and rich too." The man laughed. Allie smiled at him. "Shalimar, can you tell me what you wish to show me?"

"I wish for you, the woman in my dreams, to have my bounty." Christian wasn't sure what that might entail, but he had a feeling that if it were some of his cheese or the goats that made it, he was going to have a hard time getting them on the plane. "My dreams have foretold you coming to save us. And once you did, our people would be rich for it."

"I don't need anything. And we all helped out." Shalimar nodded and smiled. "We wanted to save the town, and that's all we wanted to do."

"Yes. I knew that you'd say that. So, when I saw you in my dreams, then in my fire, I knew that you were the woman to take my bounty back with you. You'll use it for goodness." Allie looked at him and he shrugged. "You will, will you not, my Allie? Take my bounty home and use it for others that are less fortunate?"

"If that's what you wish."

They traveled on...not far, but he could see that it was getting darker by the moment. But as soon as they got to the side of the waterway, Christian stopped. It was there, the man's bounty.

~~~

Allie sat near the big chest that was given to her. Every time she glanced at it, she would think of the elderly man and his request. She looked at Christian when he sat down beside her.

"They're going to let you take it home." She nodded and asked what the stipulations were. "None. Just the things that he asked of you. To make people's lives better than they were before. To spend what you wanted on yourself, but make sure that people are helped."

"It's a lot, don't you think?" He nodded. "I didn't know what he wanted to show me. I thought when he said bounty, he was talking about...I don't know, flowers or something. Plants, I guess."

"I would never have thought gold." She nodded and put her hand on the beautifully engraved chest that the nuggets of gold were in. "His family said that he would come down to the water daily and pan for it. Some days he'd find some, some not. But he knew, from the start, that someone was coming for it."

"Then he died." Allie took Christian's hand when he offered it. "He told me that I was to do great things with this. Then he sat down and put his hand on it and died. Right there by his bounty. It's.... He died, Christian."

"I know, love. His daughter said that he was waiting for you. That he'd made all the arrangements with her to be buried." Allie rubbed her hand over the chest again. "He made that as well, did you know?"

"His son was here a little while ago. Walker, his name was, he said that his parents had used this when they were married to put their treasures in. And when his mom passed away, his dad brought it to the water and set it up to hold more treasures. Walker said that his dad never told anyone what he found daily, just that he had good days and not so good ones."

189

Allie asked if they were still going home.

"Yes. The plane is loaded but for you and the bounty." She nodded, but just couldn't make herself get up just yet. "Honey, we can wait a few more days if you want."

"No. I'm ready to go home. But I don't want to leave him. I know that he's here still." She looked out over the water. "To think that there was this much gold in that water. It's small wonder that he wasn't robbed or killed for it."

"He was a well-respected man, and people believed him when he said someone was coming to get it." Allie said nothing. "What are you going to do with it?"

"Finish the gym my dad wanted. Hire someone to come here and put up a clinic for the people here. I know he said to use it at home, but I want this too." Christian said that was a good idea. "There are other projects, too, that we can help with. The library needs a new roof. A new playground for the school children. And food for the pantry. Those are things we talked about when we sat and talked. How there just wasn't enough food to go around."

"Those are lovely ideas. But we have to go home." She stood up then, with his help. "Mom and Dad, they're waiting on you. Brayden and I are going to put this on the plane, then we'll be going. Okay?"

"Yes, all right." She made her way to the family jet and got aboard. His mom and dad were there and she sat with them. "I'm all right. It's just been a very stressful couple of days. I'm fine now."

"I can see that. When we get home, we'll start decorating. I know that some of it has been done, but there are touches that I do each year that I'd like for you and Dane to help with." Allie told Lucy that she'd be honored. "You say that now, but you might change your mind when I tell you what it is."

"Doubtful. I'm looking forward to Christmas this year. I think for the first time in a good long time." She closed her eyes and leaned back on her seat. "I'm exhausted. I think I'll take a little nap."

She felt herself slide into sleep. It was gentle, like a small rain that came in the spring. In a vague sort of way, she knew that Christian had joined her and the rest of the family, but she was just too tired to make any effort to wake. Allie knew that if they needed her, someone would get her.

In no time, it seemed, they were home. Hours of flight didn't bother her much, as she had slept through the entire trip. She'd woken twice, when they had touched down in the States then here. Allie felt wonderfully rested and ready to face most anything. Then she remembered the chest and Joy's passing.

Finally home, she watched as the chest was put into the basement. There wasn't a safe large enough to hold it, so they were storing it there for now. No one, except the family, knew that she had it, so she figured it would be safe.

Christian met her at the top of the stairs when she went down to check on it once more.

"Everything the way it should be?" Laughing, she let him pull her into his arms. "I've missed you so much. And I love you that much more."

"We were together the entire time we were away. And it was only a week." He nuzzled her neck. "I love when you do that. I can almost feel your cat purring along my skin."

"He missed you as well." Excitement raced along her body. "How about we go in the backyard and I show you just how much he missed you?"

"It's snowing." He told her he could see that. "Won't we get cold? I mean, I know we're furred and all, but the weather

191

is nasty out."

"You're afraid to get a little snow covered?" She laughed when he did. "We are warmer than humans. I'm sure that once we get out there, you won't feel the cold. Not to mention, I have plans of warming you up."

She raced him to the door and was out in the yard seconds before he was. Just as he reached for her, she shifted into her hawk and took to the skies. It startled her when he flew beside her.

I've been practicing. She said she could see that. *I do have a bit of trouble landing, but I do all right. And Brayden finally tried. He can shift as well.*

I bet Dane is thrilled about that.

They rode the currents much like she and Dane had, letting the cool air blow them higher then lower with each breeze. When Christian landed on the top of a mountain that bordered their property, she joined him, shifting to herself when he did his cougar.

There were no words necessary. Allie stripped for him, allowing the big cat to lick her bare skin as she undressed. Christian had been right, he did warm her up. And when she was naked, the cat did the same, taking her quickly and making her come.

"Please, more." The cat knocked her to the ground and she stayed there, letting him have his fill as she screamed out each release. It excited the cougar, and she loved to make him happy. When Christian was moving up her body as his man, she held him to her as he slid deep inside of her. Their lovemaking had become gentle now. She was sure it had to do with the baby that she carried.

"I love you, Allie." She kissed him again, making sure that he knew just how much she loved him. "Everything about you, your skin, your touch. It makes me feel as if I'm the luckiest man in the world."

"I love you."

He made love to her body, touching her like he was trying to remember each inch of it. Christian tasted her skin, nipping at her then kissing the tiny wound better. The more he touched her, bringing her nearly to completion and then backing off, the more she knew that her release was going to cost her.

The snow beneath her was warming, the grass beneath it a soft comfort to her. As Christian made love to her, all she could think about was that he was hers, now and forever. And when she came, crying out his name, he did as well, filling her with more than just his seed, but his heart as well. Allie closed her eyes when it became too much for her and slipped under the darkness.

When she woke, just for a moment, she was in the bed. Christian had brought her here and wrapped her in his arms. Pulling her closer, he cupped his hand around their child and kissed her shoulder. Allie fell back to sleep feeling loved and cherished.

Alone in the bed when she woke, Allie took a shower and dressed. There was a lot to do today. There was the gold that had to be changed into money. Unpacking as well, and she wanted to see her parents. Their house, Mom told her, was done, and they were happy with Daniel cooking for them.

Christian was in the kitchen when she made her way down the stairs. "My mom is coming over in a little while. She said that you and she were going shopping."

"I forgot." He said he'd call her back. "No. Don't. I'll ask my mom to come along. Maybe Dane too."

"Dane is out of town." She knew that as well but had

forgotten. "I think she's due back in the morning. But you should take your mom. I know that mine will love spending time with her. And please, make sure that they keep the buying for the baby to a minimum. I know they won't, but see if you can try."

"I will."

She was grinning when she left to head to her mom's where Lucy was going to pick her up. Allie knew that they'd both been shopping online since they'd found out about the new addition. They'd be lucky if they had to get a single diaper, the way that they were shopping.

Chapter 15

Kendal hated doctors and he hated hospitals. But he needed help, and the only place he knew he might get help was at the clinic. He'd heard things about the place. Since Christmas, he'd been trying to work up the nerve to go there. Now he was hurting too badly to put it off any longer. So he entered, but was careful not to make anyone afraid of him.

"May I help you?" He shook his head at the little woman. "I'm sure you could use some help, young man. Just tell me what you want, and I'll try to get it for you."

"I hurt. My head hurts really bad." She asked him what he'd done. "I was in the service and they said that I was shot. I left after that, and now it hurts."

"My husband is a doctor. Can he have a look at you?" Kendal said he didn't know him. "Oh, you wouldn't, now would you? But I do, and you know me, don't you? Oh dear, I should have told you my name. I'm Lucy Stanton, my husband is Denny. Now you know him."

Kendal nodded, but had to hold onto the little woman when it made his head spin. He was lowered into a wheelchair after that, and he took her hand when she offered it. But he had to remember to not squeeze her so tightly. Closing his eyes when they started pushing him down the long hallway, he told her what his name was.

"I'm Sergeant Kendal Wayne. My unit is four-zero-seven. I have been home since July of last year, but I've been hurting since a long time before that."

Lucy said that she knew of another person that was in his unit. "His name is Captain Wilson. Do you know him?"

"Cap is here? He hurts too?" She said she didn't think so but could find out for him. "He's my friend. He told me to come here a long time ago."

"Well, you just get up in this bed and I'll go and find him for you. You just wait right here, Kendal, and I'll be back." He didn't nod this time but told her that he would. There was a pretty nurse checking his temperature for him, and she also was writing things down.

Kendal wasn't human, but she didn't seem to mind that. He was a wolf, a great gray one. But the bullet in his head, sometimes he hurt from it, and because it was there, he wasn't able to shift to make himself better. They'd told him that it was too close to his noodle, and that operating might cost him his life. Right now, he didn't care.

"I can give you something for pain once the doctor sees you." He told her that it didn't work so well on him. "I understand, Sergeant. But we have special doses for people like you."

When Lucy returned, she had Cap with her. Kendal was so glad to see his friend that he sobbed like a little baby. But Cap, he understood, and held his hand while the nurse finished up her care of him. Once she was finished, he asked Cap if he was all right.

"Yes, fine as rain. Your head hurting you again?" He said that he was sick from it. "I know, buddy. But there is little we can do about it here. The doctors here are really good, but they are probably going to tell you the same thing. You need a great surgeon to take it out."

"Hello, young man. I'm Denny Stanton. I understand that you have a headache?" He told him what was hurting, and then Cap filled him in on the rest. "A bullet in your head, huh? Well, let me have a look at it. Perhaps we can send you to a friend of mind that specializes in this sort of thing."

"I can't leave nowhere." Denny asked why not. "I got me family here, and we don't have the money for me to take off. I have me a job, if I didn't lose it by leaving today, that makes the rent, but we are strapped, sir. Pretty badly."

"You let me take care of that, son. But for now, I'm going to send you for some x-rays and a few other tests. My wife said that you were a gray wolf." He nodded. "All right then. Just be a jiffy here and we'll get things moving. In the meantime, I'm going to make a few calls and get things moving for you."

"You're in good hands now, Kendal. The best." He told Cap that he really hurt. "I know you do, but these people will help you. I know it."

Kendal was taken to x-ray a few minutes later, and while there, he heard from the nurse that his records were being sent for. He wondered how long that would take, and when he returned to his little room, the doctor was there waiting for him. And he had his records.

"I have some friends in some high places. And with your records it was easy to see why you're in so much pain." He said that they'd not been able to remove the bullet. "I understand that. And my friend, his name is Ericson O'Rourke, he's flying out first thing in the morning to talk to you. He has your records too."

"So fast." Denny said that they had the resources that made people jump when they were told. "I jump when my wife tells me to. But lately, she's so tired that I try really hard to jump before she tells me. I know that me being sick is hurting her too."

"Do you have any children, Kendal?" He said that he wasn't able to have them on account of being hurt. "I'm sorry about that. I am. I have me six sons, and two grandchildren on the way. We just found out about the second one at Christmas. A nice thing, having family around. I'm going to have someone go and pick up your wife and bring her here. That way, you can be together."

"We don't have any money. Not for her to be missing work." Again, Denny told him to leave that to him. "I don't want to have to owe you, sir. I'm behind enough as it is. We're powerful grateful for the helping, but I don't have nothing to be putting into doctoring. My head don't hurt so much now."

"Because of the medication you're getting. You just relax and we'll take care of you." Kendal wasn't sure, but he laid back. He must have dozed off, because he woke a bit later and his wife was there. Sandra, she looked worried too.

"I'm gonna see if they're gonna let me go home soon." She told him that it was all right. "Where you gonna stay? This bed ain't nearly big enough for me, much less you too."

She smiled, which was what he'd been hoping for. "Dr. Stanton put me up in a hotel, and he paid for me to have a car to come back to see you whenever I want. They're going to admit you, Kendal, and see if they can remove that thing in your head."

"It was hurting me pretty bad, honey. I don't know how much more I can take." She held his hand, and he did feel better having her there with him. When Denny came back in with an older gentleman, Doctor O'Rourke, they told him what they were going to do. "You're gonna try and take it out of me?"

"First, we're going to get you healthier. That might take us a couple of days, but once we get the ear infection that you have taken care of, we'll operate." Ericson sat down and told them what was going to happen. It was the same that the VA doctors had told him, but this guy didn't seem to think it was all a lost cause. "There will be risks involved, but I'm the best there is in operating on the brain. I want you to be assured that I'm going to do my best to make sure that once we close things up, you're going to be better."

"I've been hurting for a long time." Ericson said that he didn't doubt that. "I don't have any money for this. The insurance that we have, it's pretty poor too. My benefits for the Army, they're not good either."

"You leave that to me. I don't want you worrying. Worrying will make you stressed out, and you don't need that. Neither of you." Kendal told him thanks and he nodded. "We're going to do the best we can for you, and you're going to do the same for me. No stress and no worrying for either of you. All right?"

Kendal was put in a big room with a bed for Sandra if she wanted to spend the night. He and her had a nice meal, and they told him it was going to be his last for a little bit, so he enjoyed every bite of it. At nearly midnight, he fell asleep. Kendal, for the first time in a long time, felt better about a great many things.

~~~

Tess went over the paperwork for her grandda. He was forever losing things, and she was making sure that he was

199

covered. This trip to Ohio had taken her from her own job, but she didn't mind so much. Looking over at Ruby, her daughter, she wondered how she could sleep so soundly when there was so much going on.

"She's a joy, you know that, don't you?" Smiling at Grandda, she said she knew that and so did Ruby. "Yes, well, I love spoiling her, and you too if you'd let me."

"I'm fine, Grandda. I told you that before." He just nodded. They both knew she wasn't fine at all. "Mr. Wayne's paperwork is all complete, and I've called the VA hospital and gotten their records on him as well. Also, Captain Wilson was by, and he gave me some information on your patient as well."

"He's a good man." She said she thought they both were. "Yes. Kendal has been hurting long enough and has finally asked for some help. Unlike someone I know."

Ignoring him and his queries, she reached down and pulled the blanket up over Ruby. She would kick it off in a moment, but for now she was warm. What she wouldn't give to be able to rest like her child was.

"Tess, you should take her on over to the hotel. Everything here is ready for the surgery, and you both could use a good night's sleep. I'm glad that you were able to come with me, but there isn't any point in you being exhausted." She told him she was fine. "Tess, honey, I know that you're not, so please stop lying to me."

She looked at him and could see the concern in his eyes. And love. Patting him on the cheek and then kissing him, she reached into the playpen that held Ruby and handed her to him while she put on her coat. Tess was trying to find the right words.

"He's trying to take her from me, and then he'll have

more to hold over me. And I lost my job because he calls me several times a day or stops by and disturbs my work." He sat down with Ruby and she did as well. "We're down to our last few bucks in the bank, and that's only there because if he takes it all, the account will close to him. My rent is overdue and I have nothing to pay for my car insurance next month. Not that it matters much. He took my car out a few days ago and totaled it. And please, don't say you'll give it to me. If you do, he'll just take it again."

"Someone needs to kick his ass." She didn't disagree with him and reached for Ruby. "Does he know that you're here with me?"

"No. As far as he knows I'm still at home waiting for him to come and rob me again. Or beat me up." Grandda asked how often that happened. "A couple of times a week. Are you sorry you asked?"

"No. Are you sorry you told me?" She said that she was, sort of. "Tess, honey, I can help you with him. It's not as if he likes me any more than he does you."

"I hate him. With all that I am." Grandda nodded then got up and held her and Ruby. "He's going to hurt us. I know that he will. And because of a promise that I made, I can't do anything about it."

"I made no such promises." He walked her to the front door and helped her buckle Ruby into the car seat that had been provided with the car service. "You go on and get some rest. Tomorrow, while we're waiting on Kendal to get better, we'll talk. I know there is plenty that we can do, and he'll back off or else."

"He won't."

Grandda kissed her and she closed the door. Tess started crying the moment that the car started moving. The driver saw her, but said nothing as he handed her a box of tissues. Tess wondered if she'd ever have anyone be kind to her again.

The hotel was a very nice one. There was a crib for Ruby, much nicer than the one that she had at home. There were jars of baby food, diapers, as well as a bathing tub for Ruby. As she got her into jammies that fit her perfectly, she told her daughter what they were going to do tomorrow.

"There is a nice park that you and I are going to. Someone left you a lovely parka to put on, and a stroller. Won't that be fun?" Ruby, at six months, had no idea what she was saying, but since Tess was excited, Ruby was as well. "Then we're going to have a nice dinner with the Stanton family. Great-Grandda said they're the nicest people he's ever met. That will be very different for us, since we don't know any nice people but him."

Ruby giggled and Tess took her to the rocker and held her while she laid her head on her shoulder. Ruby was hers, and the only thing in the world that kept her going all the time. Without her, Tess was sure that she would have ended her misery months ago.

When she was sleeping, Tess put her in the crib. Turning on the nightlight, she made her way to the living area and sat on the plush couch. This was wonderful, she thought, and stretched out on it to watch television. At some point she must have dozed off, because Grandda woke her when he came home at midnight.

"I'm sorry I woke you, honey." She told him it was fine and stood up. "I want you to know that I've hired someone to keep an eye on you while you're here. Dexter might not know where you are now, but he will know where I am soon enough."

"You didn't have to do that." He said that he did. He

loved her. "I love you too, Grandda. More than anything. But Dexter won't like you interfering."

"He'll just have to get over it." She nodded and made her way to the bedroom that she shared with Ruby. "Good night, Tess. See you in the morning."

Telling him good night, she checked on her daughter and got into bed. Her cell phone started ringing almost as soon as she turned her light off. It was Dexter.

"Where the fuck are you?" She didn't answer him. "Tess, I swear to Christ, you'd better be on your way home. So help me, I'm sick of your shit."

"Stay away from me, Dexter. I will call the police again." He screamed at her that she'd better not and Tess closed the connection. He'd call back in a few minutes, so she turned her phone off.

Crying herself into a fitful sleep, she wondered what she'd done to deserve this sort of treatment. Dexter hadn't always been like this. When they were children, he was a model child. Then when her mom died about five years ago, he decided that she was going to be his punching bag. No matter what she did, it was all wrong. Then she'd gotten pregnant with Ruby.

"How could you?" She told him that it's what happened when someone was planning to get married. "You can't have this kid. I won't allow it. Get rid of it."

"I'm happy I'm going to have a baby, Dexter. You're going to be an uncle. And Kenneth is happy too. We planned this." Dexter slapped her, hard enough that she hit her head on the table and it knocked her out. When she woke, the police were there and her world turned upside down.

"Ms. O'Rourke, I'm afraid there has been an accident. Your fiance was killed."

She didn't know what had happened or how he died, but she knew as surely as she sat there with an ice pack on her face that Dexter had done it. And she was next.

Paranormal Romance with a Bite!

BLOOD, BODY AND MIND:
A KATHI S. BARTON PARANORMAL ROMANCE

YOUR FREE COPY IS WAITING...

Aaron MacManus, the new master vampire of the realm just wanted to go out and meet some of his subjects and to figure out what needed to be done to set things right.

April and Demetrius Carlovetti own an air service and are the most trusted and well liked vampires in Aaron's realm. What he didn't expect when he visited them was betrayal. His own bodyguards try to murder him and blame it on the Carlovetti's.

Sara Temple was not a vampire. She pilots planes for the Carlovetti Airways. She had secrets of her own and working for this small air service is keeping her out of sight. The last thing she wanted to do was save a vampire, even an extremely good looking one.

Sara was only trying to survive but with Aaron she becomes embroiled in politics, the magic of several realms involving a queen in peril, magical beings, passion and love.

Blood, Body and Mind, the first book in the Aaron's Kiss series.

Get Your Free Book!

http://eepurl.com/brCBvP

Before You Go...

HELP AN AUTHOR

write a review

THANK YOU!

Share your voice and help guide other readers to these wonderful books. Even if it's only a line or two your reviews help readers discover the author's books so they can continue creating stories that you'll love. Login to your favorite retailer and leave a review. Thank you.

AWARD WINNING, BESTSELLING AUTHOR

Kathi Barton, winner of the Pinnacle Book Achievement award as well as a best-selling author on Amazon and All Romance books, lives in Nashport, Ohio with her husband Paul. When not creating new worlds and romance, Kathi and her husband enjoy camping and going to auctions. She can also be seen at county fairs with her husband who is an artist and potter.

Her muse, a cross between Jimmy Stewart and Hugh Jackman, brings her stories to life for her readers in a way that has them coming back time and again for more. Her favorite genre is paranormal romance with a great deal of spice. You can visit Kathi online and drop her an email if you'd like. She loves hearing from her fans. aaronskiss@gmail.com.

Follow Kathi on her blog: http://kathisbartonauthor.blogspot.com/

www.ingramcontent.com/pod-product-compliance
Lightning Source LLC
Chambersburg PA
CBHW021958190626
46808CB00017B/2131